ILE DE DESPOIR

A NOVEL

A.D. PLAUTZ

ISBN: 979-8-89031-955-5 (sc)
ISBN: 979-8-89031-956-2 (hc)
ISBN: 979-8-88640-046-5 (e)

Because of the dynamic nature of the Internet, any web addresses or links contained in this book may have changed since publication and may no longer be valid. The views expressed in this work are solely those of the author and do not necessarily reflect the views of the publisher, and the publisher hereby disclaims any responsibility for them.

THE EWINGS
PUBLISHING

One Galleria Blvd., Suite 1900, Metairie, LA 70001
(504) 702-6708

A Sequel to "The Dreamer 4"

Other Novels by A. D. Plautz:

The Dreamer 4 (April 2023)

The Interrupted Traveler (May 2023)

Review of The Interrupted Traveler:

Readers of this smart, lively yarn will enjoy watching an ordinary guy show how extraordinary he can be with the right challenges. On a sad family errand to the South Pacific, Ron Pritchard must first survive a plane crash on a remote, uninhabited island, then look after the other survivors – a hot pop star and her entourage – while waiting for rescuers. But a vicious crew of drug smugglers is also searching for the lost plane... Each new crisis forces Ron to analyze cooly but empathize passionately. This book is a genuine, compulsive page-turner.

-Joe Sanders, veteran thriller reviewer for *Publishers Weekly*

PROLOGUE

*H*e put the body behind a large tree. He looked down on the body. She was still naked but he didn't care. He stacked her clothes next to her but kept the purse. It was supposed to snow tomorrow so with any luck she would be covered with snow and maybe not found until spring. He carefully backed away from the tree and walked out of the dense forest. They had a date earlier that evening but it had not turned out well. When he suggested that they go to his place for a nightcap, she turned away and said no. He became angry and struck her from behind. He dragged her to the car and went to his apartment. When he had her there, she started to come to. He was on top of her and she fought to get free. He struck her several times in the face and then raped her as she cried. Afterward she was still crying silently and he strangled her with his hands. He had killed before and did not feel any remorse. He had made the mistake of thinking she was similar to the girl he was obsessed with.

CHAPTER 1

SUNDAY NIGHT

It was a cold December night. Ron Pritchard looked at the document. It was in a picture frame and covered with glass. It said that he now had a Bachelor's Degree in Engineering. It had been a long four years but he finally had it. During that time, he had met his future wife, Susan. They had had a strange summer in which he had been in a terrible car crash that had almost killed him. Sue had stayed by him the whole time as he slowly healed into an almost normal condition. The healed broken leg still bothered him somewhat but he could limp around ok. Now that he had finally graduated, he had a good job offer from an aerospace company. He was scheduled to start to work in a week, but today was a day to celebrate. It was a party, a small gathering of Ron's friends held at his landlord's place. Ron had the efficiency apartment upstairs but it was too small for even this small gathering of friends. His landlord, Matt and his wife Becky decided to throw a party for Ron. Sue and her roommate Joan were present as was Joan's boyfriend Jerry Baker. George Coleman, the college campus police chief and his girlfriend Jennifer were also there. Andy Hall, one of George's patrolmen and his girlfriend Sasha, were also in attendance. At first Sasha was rather uncomfortable about attending the party since she and Andy were the only African Americans present. That changed very quickly since everyone greeted her warmly and she could see that they were all very close friends. Beer and pizza were the mainstays of the party although soft drinks and chips were also available. Becky had also baked a chocolate cake for the occasion.

Ron could not believe it, all of his friends were in attendance, and every one of the people he loved was here. Ron had no immediate family since he had been an only child when his parents had died in a car accident. Now he was engaged to Sue and his future looked bright. He was somewhat concerned about the new job, but it was the same place he had been a co-op at a year ago, so he figured he should be ok. For now, Ron had a week off now to spend with Sue who was still a freshman at the college. Sue cornered him in the kitchen as he was getting a beer from the refrigerator.

"So, what are we doing this week? Classes don't start for another two weeks for me."

Ron looked at her. "Well, we could just relax and have some quiet time."

"How about we visit my parents place?" she asked. He had not been able to visit her parents earlier because of the car accident that had hospitalized him for some time. When he got out of the hospital he had to study hard to complete his course work to graduate.

"I suppose we could do that," he reluctantly replied.

"Good. I want to show off my engagement ring." Her eyes sparkled. To Ron, Sue was the most beautiful girl he had ever known. She was about two inches shorter than his six-foot frame, had bright green eyes and was a brunette. Tonight, she was wearing one of her blue dresses that accentuated her slim figure.

"Ok. We could leave tomorrow for a short stay. I need to get up to Cleveland and find an apartment anyway." Ron was planning on staying weekdays near his new job and returning to see her at the college campus on the weekends.

"Can you afford to keep two apartments?" She asked.

"Actually, with my new salary and my trust fund I can afford another efficiency apartment and still set some money aside in savings," he explained.

"Ok. I'll go along with that, as long as you are here on weekends," she agreed.

George, his best friend, came into the kitchen to talk to Ron. George wasn't wearing his police chief uniform and was dressed casual for a change with jeans and a sport shirt.

"Ron….can I show you something?" he asked.

"Sure. What is it?" Ron asked. Sue was curious and moved closer also.

George took a small box from his pocket and opened it. It contained a diamond ring.

"I was planning on asking Jennifer to marry me tonight, but didn't want take anything away from your graduation party." George blushed.

"Wow, that's great. Go ahead and ask her." Ron smiled. George had been dating Jen for a few months now and she appeared to be a perfect match for him.

"Good," Sue replied. "I know she is in love with you, George." Ron and Sue had double dated with George and Jennifer several times and the girls had become fast friends. They all went into the front room where Matt, Ron's landlord and the home owner, was explaining a joke to everybody. Everyone was laughing and having a good time. George walked over to Jennifer who was a cute petite blonde wearing a red pants suit and stopped in front of her with a solemn look on his face. Everyone stopped laughing, wondering what George was doing.

"What is it George?" Jen asked with a curious look on her face.

"Jennifer…" George got down on one knee, "Will you marry me?" He offered her the open box with the ring. Jennifer looked at him with a funny look on her face as tears started to run down her cheek.

"Yes, Yes, yes!" she answered as she got down with him and hugged him. Everyone in the room began to cheer. He put the ring on her finger and they kissed. Matt and Becky began to clap and so did everyone else. Ron was happy for George and offered a toast with his beer bottle held high. Sasha looked at Andy with a curious expression on her face. Andy looked at her and said "Hey, I didn't know he was going to do this." Joan and Jerry were off to one side and Joan looked at Jerry. She whispered, "Don't you get any ideas, buster." Jerry was a fourth-year sophomore at the college and was a long way from graduation yet.

"Ok," Jerry replied with some relief. Joan and Sue were both freshmen with a long way to go to graduate. Joan had started to date Jerry last summer and they were going steady. Joan's main goal was to complete college but she wanted to have some fun on the side. Jerry was an officer in a fraternity but had started to take college more seriously after he met Joan.

After a while, the party died down as people started to head home. Ron and Sue stayed to help Matt and Becky clean up. Matt had been married to Becky for six years but they didn't have any children yet. He worked as a mechanic in a service station and she did tax preparation on the side. Matt had renovated the upper floor of their house as an efficiency apartment to raise a little extra cash from college students since they were only about a mile from the campus. Ron was their first tenant and they had forged a strong bond of friendship and trust with him. It was getting late and Ron asked Matt if it was ok to break the rules this one time and let him have an overnight guest. Sue and Ron were engaged to be married anyway.

"Yes, I guess it's alright tonight," Matt replied. He knew that Ron had celebrated a little too much and did not want him to drive Sue back to the dorm in his condition. Sue was still sober but had not driven Ron's Corvette yet. Truth be told, she was a little scared of all of the horsepower that the vehicle had.

"Thanks." Ron slurred his words slightly. "I really appreciated the party." Ron was happy. He was about to start a new phase of his life and had secured the love of his life with Sue. Ron and Sue climbed the outside stairs up to his apartment after everything was cleaned up and they had said goodnight to Matt and Becky. They kissed as they got inside, but Ron stumbled over to the bed and was fast asleep before Sue could get undressed. So, she cuddled up with him and hoped he did not snore too loud. She was thinking about her visit to her family and hoped Ron would get along with her stepfather.

CHAPTER 2

Ron woke up with a terrible hangover. Too many beers, he thought as he got up. Sue was sleeping on the couch in the living room. She had moved when he started to snore loudly. He did not want to disturb her, so he went into the bathroom and took a shower. Afterwards he dressed and felt better. He wore his typical khaki pants and a warm blue flannel shirt. Sue was already up and dressed. She had jeans and a sweater on. She was looking in the refrigerator for something to cook for breakfast but it was empty.

"Don't you have any food?" she asked as he came into the kitchen.

"I didn't shop this week, just bought the beer for the party," he responded. He took some aspirin down from a shelf and swallowed a couple with a glass of water. "Let's go to the diner down the street...I'll buy you breakfast."

"Ok." She turned to kiss him. This typically led to a more physical response, but he was too hungry to bed her. She was in a hurry to visit her parents today so she didn't mind. Classes were over for the semester with a Christmas break starting this week. It was turning colder outside but had not snowed yet.

"I have to change out the Corvette for the Jeep. The weather prediction is for snow tonight," he commented.

"Yeah, I suppose that's a good idea," she said, picking up her coat. She had figured that he would switch out the Corvette for the Jeep for the cold weather. The four wheel drive Jeep would be better on winter roads. It was a short walk down the street to the small diner. They were quiet during the walk; he was still suffering with the hangover; she was thinking about going home for a week.

"I told Joan that we could maybe give her a ride back home," she noted as they sat down at a table in the diner. "I hope that's ok." Joan was from the same city they were driving to.

"Sure. There's plenty of room in the Jeep," he responded. They ordered breakfast.

CHAPTER 3

Andy Hall was driving one of the campus police cars, making his daily rounds of the campus. It was a little after nine in the morning. Almost everyone had left for the Christmas break so he was not expecting any excitement. The weather was very windy and cool, in the 50s and very overcast with heavy gray clouds. A cold front was moving in. If it got much colder tonight it would probably snow.

As he turned into the drive by the Student Union he thought he saw something red in the woods adjacent to the building. It was probably just some debris blown in by the wind. Still, he figured that he better check it out. He parked the squad car and walked into the woods. The red item turned out to be a woman's skirt caught on a branch of a tree probably blown there by the wind. "*What the heck?*" he thought as he walked closer. He thought he saw something on the other side of the tree. As he walked past the tree he saw a body. It was a woman lying face down on the ground, totally nude. He stepped back in shock. "Oh my God!" he whispered. He knew better than to disturb a crime scene but had to see if she was still alive. He held his hand to her neck but there was no pulse and the body was cold. He ran back to the car and got on the radio. He turned on the police flasher lights.

"George!" he almost screamed into the mike, "You need to get over to the Student Union as soon as possible!"

"What's up?" George Coleman replied. He was the only one in the office today since the other two members of the small campus police force were out for the weekend and he was doing dispatch duty.

"I...I found a body...she's dead," Andy stammered. "We need to alert the city police!"

"Jesus," George exclaimed. His mind was racing. He never had a killing on the college campus and hoped this was just an accident. He grabbed his coat and ran to the other police car. As he started it up he called the city police and informed them that a body had been found and that they should get to the campus. The drive to the Student Union was only a short distance from the campus police station so he was on the scene in only a couple of minutes. He parked behind Andy's squad car and saw Andy sitting in the car in the passenger seat with the passenger door open.

"Where is it?" he asked Andy who appeared to be in shock.

"Over in the woods....I'll show you." Andy got up reluctantly and led George to the body.

"Oh My God!" George whispered. "Is she dead?"

"Yeah...no pulse and it's cold."

George examined the body. There were marks on the girl's neck. It appeared that she had been strangled. He didn't want to disturb it until the city police forensic people arrived. From the view he had, the girl sort of looked like Ron's Sue, same slim body, same color hair and style as Ron's fiancée. From what he could see of the face, it looked like she had been beaten badly. He took out his cell phone and dialed Ron.

"Hello?" Ron answered from the diner.

"Ron...do you happen to know where Sue is?" George calmly asked.

"Yes...she is sitting across from me. Do you need to talk to her?" Ron answered.

"Oh good...no... I don't need to talk to her." George was relieved.

"What's going on?" Ron asked. As a police auxiliary officer for the campus police force, he was immediately interested.

George hesitated. "We found the body of a girl. She kind of looks a lot like Sue."

"Oh no…. do you need me to help?" Ron was shocked.

"No. The city police are here; I think they will have jurisdiction on something like this."

"OK. Let me know if there is anything I can do," Ron said, relieved. Sue was looking at Ron with a curious look on her face.

"What's the matter?" she asked, seeing the look of bad news on Ron's face.

"The police found the body of a girl on campus," he stated plainly.

"Oh no….do they know who it was?" she asked.

"Not yet," Ron replied. They finished their breakfast and returned to Ron's apartment. Ron had to switch the Corvette for the Jeep and he wanted Sue to come along with him. With a possible murderer running loose he did not want to leave her alone. After switching out the cars at his storage garage, they drove over to her dormitory to pick up Joan and Sue's stuff.

Joan was wearing blue jeans and a yellow sweatshirt. She noticed that Ron and Sue were somewhat subdued and asked "What's the matter?"

"The police found the body of a girl on campus," Sue said.

"Was it a student?" Joan was concerned.

"We don't know yet. George will fill me in later I'm sure," Ron replied as he picked up their suitcases full of stuff they were taking home. He walked out of the dorm room to take these down to the Jeep.

Joan turned to Sue. " Is Ron going to have to stay and help?"

"No. George told him the city police will do the investigation. I am worried though if there is a killer on campus," Sue replied.

"I hope that's not the case." Joan was worried. Next semester it would be getting dark early and she did have a late afternoon class to attend. Walking alone in the dark was not a pleasant thought if there was predator on campus attacking young women. Joan was an attractive brown-haired girl, not as tall as Sue but very pretty. She had been Sue's best friend since high school and was her roommate in the dorm. She feared running into the killer as much as the rest of the women at the college.

CHAPTER 4

The 3-hour trip north to Cleveland was boring and normal, they missed the rush hour traffic so they got to Strongsville in pretty good time. The talk in the car was somewhat subdued. Sue and Joan talked about their class schedules for the upcoming semester. They did have a couple of classes together since one was an elective, the other a requirement. Sue also had to take chemistry and was counting on Ron's help with such a difficult class. Since he would be working in Cleveland and only back on campus on weekends she hoped he would spend time helping her. Ron was quiet, thinking about the new engineering job he was starting at the Newmatic Company. Also, he was thinking about the call from George. If there was a predator on campus he felt he should be around to protect Sue. Sue did have a third degree black belt in karate (he'd witnessed her take down a mugger with one kick when they were dating), but she was vulnerable if someone snuck up behind her. They dropped Joan off at her parent's house and headed over to Sue's house. It was Ron's first visit to Sue's parents since they became engaged. It would be a long engagement since Sue wanted to finish college before getting married. That was ok with Ron. Although he was madly in love with her, he wanted time to get established with the new job before they started married life together.

"Your parents know we are coming, right?" he asked.

"Yes. They have the spare room all fixed up for you," Sue purred. "It's right next to mine," she laughed.

"Well, that's convenient," he noted. He and Sue had been sexually active for several months. He was sure that the parents would not want them to share a room, even though they were engaged.

"I hope you can survive my two rotten brothers," she noted. Her brothers were spoiled brats who often pulled pranks on her at the most inconvenient times. They were twins and about eight years younger than Sue.

"Maybe I can reason with them," he postulated.

"Good luck with that." Sue smiled.

CHAPTER 5

It had turned colder and was beginning to snow. George Coleman walked over to the two city police detectives. They introduced themselves as Chris Johnson and Wayne Kent. They were both wearing overcoats with business suits and ties. They had examined the body and then let the forensic people have her.

"Did you find any identification on her at all?" Detective Kent asked George.

"No, just a few items of clothing," George answered.

"Well, the CSI guy tells me she was probably killed last night sometime between nine o'clock and midnight. It's difficult to make a more accurate time with this cold weather. She appears to have been raped but she obviously fought back," Chris Johnson replied. "There is evidence of particles under her fingernails so we should be able to get a DNA sample of her killer. Did you notice the two burn marks on her back?"

"No, I guess I missed that," George noted.

'Yeah, there were two small punctures in two places. Apparently her attacker used a high voltage stun device to paralyze her. Those things basically immobilize the victim."

"Wow, aren't those devices only used by police?" George asked.

"No, you can buy them at any gun show now. They are typically sold as self-defense items for women," Detective Kent replied. "We'll know more when we get a report from the morgue after an autopsy."

"Ok. I guess you guys will be doing the investigating on this," George noted.

"Yeah, we will work it. You can help by seeing if anyone is reported missing on campus."

"I can do that. Let me know if there is anything else I can do," George agreed.

"We will keep you in the loop if we find out anything," Detective Kent responded.

George watched the detectives leave as the victim was loaded into a police van and driven back to the city. He walked over to Andy Hall who was standing next to his police car.

"George, I never saw anything like this on our campus before," Andy said.

"Well, I guess it has happened now," George looked down. The college campus was near the city but was a small college with only about nine thousand students. At least this happened on Christmas break, so most of the students had gone home for the holiday. Maybe he could find out if it was a missing college student. Andy was apparently still shaken up. The campus police force basically only wrote parking tickets and broke up the occasional problem of drunken students fighting at a wild party. He told Andy to take the rest of the day off, then drove back to the police office. As he parked the car and walked toward the office he saw a young girl wearing a brown coat sitting in the small office waiting area. He walked in and hung up his coat as the girl stood up and approached.

"Can I help you miss?" he asked.

"It's about my roommate. We are in Spenser Hall and were going to drive home today but she didn't come home from her date last night." The girl had a worried look on her face.

"Does she typically stay out all night?" he asked. He was hoping it was not the victim.

"Never; she always comes back to the dorm before curfew," she explained. "I tried to call her cell phone several times but got no response."

"What is your name?" He led her over to his desk and had her sit down.

"Sheila, Sheila Cook," she answered.

"And the name of your roommate?" He was writing this down on a tablet.

"Cindy Carlson."

"Do you happen to know who she was with last night?" George started to think it was the victim.

"She didn't say. Just that she had met a guy in the Student Union and that he asked her out," Sheila responded. "We were going to leave last night but she postponed it to today so she could make the date."

"Do you have a recent picture of her?" George asked.

"Yes." She dug out her cell phone from the small purse she had. "We took this selfie last week when we went to the winter concert." She showed him the picture. It sure looked like the girl in the forest. She had the same hair style, green eyes and very pretty.

"Can you send me that photo?" He gave her his cell phone number.

"Is something wrong?' she asked noticing his sad look.

"Can you check back at your dorm room to see if she maybe came in after you left?" he asked. I will contact you if we find out anything, OK?" George replied. "Maybe the battery in her phone is low and maybe she decided to stay out with her date. It happens a lot on campus."

"Cindy would have let me know. I'm worried," Sheila replied.

"I understand. I will let you know the minute I find out anything." He didn't want to upset the girl until he had a positive ID on the victim. "Did she have any identifying marks or tattoos?" he asked.

"Yes, she had a small tattoo of a heart with a lightning bolt thru it on her ankle. She got it after a particularly bad break up with her old boyfriend," Sheila noted.

"Do you know the boyfriend's name?" he asked.

"His name was John something…but he's not at this college."

"Ok. Thanks for coming in. I will start looking for her. Let me know if she shows up at the dorm?

"Sure." She got up and walked out into the snowstorm.

George called the detectives. Detective Kent answered. He informed the detective that a girl had come into his office about a missing roommate. He asked if there was a tattoo on the victim's leg. Detective Kent looked at the preliminary report he had from the CSI guys.

"Yes. There is a heart tattoo on her left ankle," Kent replied.

"Ok. I believe I have the victim's name. It may be Cindy Carlson. She went on a date last night and never returned to her dorm room. Pending an official identification, I believe it to be her."

"Good work. We will need to talk to the roommate. And can you contact a parent or someone to make a positive ID?" Kent asked.

"Yeah, I will look at the campus records in the computer to get you a home address. By the way…she had a recent breakup with a boyfriend named John. It might be good to talk to him also. The roommate could not remember his last name but maybe her parents would know." George was happy to help the detectives. "I'll send you the girl's picture I got from the roommate."

CHAPTER 6

MONDAY AFTERNOON

It had snowed quite a bit on the way to Cleveland but the roads were only wet, not covered with snow. Ron pulled into the driveway at Sue's parents' house. He parked the red Jeep behind a blue Toyota SUV. The house was a two-story colonial with white siding and gray roof. It had a two car garage and a nice manicured lawn. As he got out and moved to the back to get Sue's suitcase, the front door opened and Sue's mother came rushing out to greet them.

"You guys made good time," she said as she hugged Sue.

"So nice to be home," Sue replied.

Ron had Sue's suitcase as he walked up to her mother. "Hello Mrs. Parker," he greeted her with a smile.

"Hello Ron." She looked at him. She noticed he walked with a slight limp, a result of the car accident last summer. "Are you alright?" she asked.

"Just fine," he replied.

"Well, come inside out of the cold." She led them to the door.

"Nice place you have here," he remarked, looking at the great room with a nice big fireplace. The room and stairs were carpeted with a thick pile carpet.

"Yes, we like it," she answered. "Your room will be the last room on the right." As they climbed the stairs to the second floor she said, "Your room is just across from the boy's room. The bathroom is the second door on the left. Dinner is at six." As she turned to go back down stairs, Ron turned to say something to Sue, but she had entered her bedroom with the suitcase. He opened the door to his assigned room and looked in. It was a simple small bedroom with a twin bed, a desk and a chest of drawers. A curtained window looked out over the backyard. He was taking off his coat when the door to the boy's room opened and an eleven year old boy wearing blue jeans and a red T-shirt walked over to him with his hand out.

"Hi, my name is Damien," he said as he came close to Ron.

"Hello." Ron turned with a smile and held his hand out to shake hands. Instead of shaking hands, Damien brought up his knee up into Ron's groin in an attempt to disable him. Ron was quicker and turned just enough that the intended knee crashed into the inside of his left thigh.

Damien's eyes got wide as he thought he had delivered a disabling blow and Ron did not collapse. Ron grabbed him by the throat and pushed him against the wall.

"It's nice to meet you," Ron said as he applied pressure to the boy's throat.

"Wait!" Damien cried out as he struggled to get free.

"Just remember… I can crush you like an insect," Ron hissed.

Sue came around the corner and looked in. "Oh, I see you met one of my idiot brothers. Please don't kill him now. My parents will get upset. Wait until later," Sue implored.

"Ok. As long as you say so." Ron said menacingly as he released the small boy. Damien looked at both of them with fear in his eyes, ran to his room and slammed the door shut. Sue and Ron just laughed softly. She walked over to Ron's bedroom door and closed it and turned back to Ron. They kissed passionately for a couple of minutes and then parted.

"Are they both that bad?" Ron asked as they sat on his bed.

"Well, Donald is a little worse, but yeah they are both pretty terrible," Sue explained. "They are always playing pranks on me like pouring syrup in my hair as I am getting ready to go out for a date."

"Wow, seems like they need some discipline. Maybe I can do something about it?" Ron replied.

"Just don't let my stepfather see you. He thinks they are his little angels," Sue noted. "We better get downstairs or my parents will think we are doing something up here."

'Well, we are." Ron kissed her again. They got up and headed down stairs.

CHAPTER 7

George Coleman looked up Cindy Carlson in the campus directory and got her home address and home phone number. He called the parents and asked them to visit the city morgue to make a positive identification. Normally he would have made a personal visit to their house to give them the bad news, but he was still unsure of the victim's identity. He asked them to call Detective Kent who was taking the lead on this case. He did drive over to Spenser Hall and checked with Sheila to determine if Cindy had returned. Sheila still had no word from Cindy. He asked her to sit down and he told her about the body they found. She broke down crying and asked him who could have hurt her roommate. He said that the police were looking into it. He asked her if there was anything else she could remember about Cindy's date. She could not remember anything except that they were going to go out to dinner. That gave George an idea. He could check out the local restaurants to see if anyone remembered seeing Cindy and her date. He thanked Sheila and said he was sorry about her roommate but that the police were going to find the guy who did this. He left the dorm and walked through the snow that was starting to accumulate. He drove back to the police station and as he parked the car his cell phone rang.

"George, what can you tell me about what happened?" It was Ron calling from Cleveland.

"Hi Ron. Well, we think we know who the victim is and she was a student. We know that she had a date last night but did not return to her dorm room. Her roommate says that the victim told her that they were going out for dinner. So that gives me a start on places to look," George replied.

"Boy, I should be there helping you," Ron noted with a sigh.

"No…you enjoy your visit up north. We can handle things here. The city detectives are working this case," George replied.

"Ok. I have to go now and have dinner with Sue's parents." Ron hung up. George was always amazed at Ron trying to help out. Ron had helped the police catch and prosecute a rapist on campus last summer. Ron was the kind of guy that always tried to help out whenever possible. George was glad that he was part of the police force as an auxiliary. It was a voluntary position and did not pay anything, but Ron did not need the money; he just sort of always helped out.

CHAPTER 8

Dinner with the Parkers was somewhat subdued. Mrs. Parker had fixed fried chicken and macaroni and cheese. This was one of the favorites of Donald and Darien. Ron was not surprised. The twin boys seemed to be very spoiled. Most of the conversation was between Sue and her mother. Sue was talking about her classes next semester and her mother seemed very interested. Mr. Parker merely smiled and ate quietly. Darien scowled at Ron most of the meal but behaved himself. Donald tried to kick Ron under the table but got a harder kick in return. He jumped in surprise but did not say anything. After dinner Sue and her mother did the cleanup and the twins went downstairs to the finished basement to play video games. Ron and Mr. Parker moved to the great room and sat on the Barcalounger and couch. Mr. Parker lit the fireplace. It was a gas-log type and turned on with a switch. There was a large flat TV against the inside wall but Mr. Parker did not turn it on. Instead, he turned to Ron.

"So, you are really going to marry Sue?" he asked.

"Yes…we plan to do it after she graduates," Ron stated.

"That's four years away. Can you wait that long?"

"Well, that is what she wants to do," Ron replied.

"I understand you have a job up here in Cleveland and she is still going to be on campus," Mr. Parker noted. "That makes for a long-distance relationship. Those usually don't work out."

"It may be difficult but I will still see her on weekends," Ron answered.

"Why did you ask her to marry you?" Mr. Parker asked.

"Well…we are in love and I did not want to lose her. She is the smartest, nicest and most beautiful girl I have ever met," Ron answered.

"I assume you are intimate with her. Why buy the cow when you can get the milk for free?" Mr. Parker smiled at Ron.

"It was the honorable thing to do. Besides I cannot see living without her in my life," Ron answered again. Ron did not care for this line of questioning but he could see that it was something a parent would do.

"I don't think that this will work out. She will probably get hurt in the long run." Mr. Parker was thinking of his wife who got pregnant, had a baby and then a divorce when the father of the baby abandoned her. He did not want a similar fate for Sue. He had met her mother six years later and they had a very happy marriage, but the previous six years of raising a child and working to support it had been very hard on his wife.

"I am totally dedicated to Sue. If for some reason we separate it will because she wants to, not me." Ron was becoming defensive.

"That's what you say now. Tell me the same thing three years from now and we will gladly plan the wedding." Mr. Parker noted that he had touched a nerve in the boy. Ron got up and walked to the door and stepped outside. He had to cool down. He understood what Mr. Parker was saying but did not believe that it would turn out that way.

"Where is Ron?" Sue asked as she entered the great room.

"We were talking and he got up and went outside," her stepfather answered. "Do you actually expect him to wait four years for you to graduate?" he asked her.

"That is what we agreed to," Sue replied. Apparently Ron and her stepfather had had an argument.

"You know it won't work out with you being separated by 200 miles," her step father said stiffly.

"You don't know that. We are in love," she replied.

"Love…as if you knew what that was. You have only known each other for six months. You barely know him. Men are not like you think," he said quietly.

"I know him better than you think." Sue was starting to tear up.

"You have already been intimate with him, and it has blinded you to this situation," he said.

"Why are you so against us?" she pleaded as she walked to the door and went outside. It was cold but Ron was not wearing a coat and was standing on the porch looking out at the road.

"Are you alright?" she asked as she walked up to him and put her arm around him.

"I guess so…maybe your father is right," he sighed.

"Please don't say that. We have a plan and we can work it out," she said.

"Look. I do love you and don't want to lose you." He turned to her and pulled her close to him.

"I know. Life is complicated sometimes but we can make it work," Sue replied. "Ok. I believe we can make it work. What does your mother say?" he asked.

"She likes you. She told me about her experiences with her first love and resulting divorce, but she does not see that happening to us," Sue answered.

"That's good. Let's go inside and get out of the cold," he replied. "Can I use your laptop to get on the internet to check out apartments near my new job?"

"Sure. Let's use the dining room table. It's all cleared off now." Sue turned to go back inside and he followed. They walked through the great room but her stepfather did not pay attention as he was reading the Cleveland Plain Dealer newspaper.

CHAPTER 9

George Coleman was in the police office early. He had called the rest of his staff and deputies to come in even though the campus was on Christmas break. He assigned Andy Hall and another deputy to check out several local restaurants with the photo of the victim. Earlier he had a call from Detective Wayne Kent who reported that the parents had made a positive identification of the victim, Cindy Carlson. The preliminary autopsy showed that the girl had been raped and had fought for her life. Traces of skin under her fingernails had provided a DNA sample. There were traces of tape on her arms where the killer had taped her arms behind her back. The city police had not yet found a match to the DNA in their preliminary search of databases and they were considering sending a request to the FBI to have them search their database. The snow had pretty much melted away since the temperature was in the forties and the sun was shining. George walked over to the Student Union. It was still open but only had a skeleton crew working. He looked for Simon, the food court manager. Since there was not much business, he was working the grill making breakfast for a couple of remaining students. George caught his attention and Simon walked over to George after serving the two students.

"Hi George, what's up?" he asked.

"I don't suppose you have heard of our latest crime?" George asked.

"I heard something about a young girl that was found dead," Simon replied.

"Yeah. I was hoping you could look at her photo and see if you recognize her. She supposedly met her killer here in the student union," George noted as he showed him the girl's photo.

"Wow, she is pretty. You know we see a lot of students in here. She does look familiar but I cannot say anything more than that." Simon handed George back the photo.

"You don't have video surveillance here, do you?"

"No, if the kids knew they were being recorded they would go elsewhere for their snacks," Simon replied.

"Yeah, that was what I thought." George showed some disappointment. "Well, thanks anyway." He turned to go.

"You better catch this guy soon, no one wants a killer on campus," Simon shouted after George. George was hoping to keep the killing quiet for a while so he could look for the killer, but somehow it got on the six o'clock news last night. The college did not need this type of reputation.

CHAPTER 10

*H*e had watched the news. He was disappointed that the body was found so quickly. He had hoped that he would have more time to put his plan into place. He had already determined that his prey had gone home for the Christmas break. Still, it could work out. He had time to find at least one or two other victims to select before he moved on to the one he obsessed on. The police would assume it was a serial killer doing the killings. Then he would make his move and they would waste their time trying to find the body. He pulled out his cell phone and called his sister.

"Hi Sis. How's it going?" he asked

"Oh…hi. Everything is good," she responded.

"Did you get the job?" he asked.

"Yes, better than I expected. I got the executive secretary position."

"Perfect," he said. "You know what to do?" he asked.

"Yes, we already discussed it. I know what to do…but I still don't think she is worth it," she replied.

"I need this. You have to help," he implored.

"I know. Still, I don't really need the job, we are rich enough already."

"Just do your part. I will make it worth your while," he replied.

"Ok. No problem." She hung up.

He smiled. Everything was working out. They had worked together before to get their parent's estate. The police had no clue then, they wouldn't figure this out either. The girl he wanted was worth it. She had rejected him once; he would make her pay. She would have to beg him for it.

CHAPTER 11

Ron Pritchard had looked at a couple of small efficiency apartments in a Polish neighborhood near the Newmatic Company plant. He settled for a second story walk up that was located over a hardware store. It was a sparse single room efficiency with a single bed, closet, chest of drawers, a table with two chairs, a hot plate and microwave on a kitchen counter with a sink and a small refrigerator. A small bathroom with a toilet and small shower was also in one corner of the room, separated by a six foot wall and a door. The parking was behind the building so he had to walk around the hardware store to get to the entrance that led to the stairs up to the apartment. A small Polish restaurant was around the other corner that served a breakfast and lunchtime crowd. Both the hardware store and the restaurant were closed in the evening so it was relatively quiet. It wasn't much, but the rent was cheap enough. He was warned by the landlord that the neighborhood got rough at night with gang members ruling the streets. The best thing was it was only a block from his new job so he could walk to work in the morning. He paid a months' rent in advance along with a security deposit. He brought Sue to see the apartment the next day and she looked around the room.

"It's not much, is it," she noted as she surveyed the room. It had one window that looked out to the back of the building where his Jeep was parked.

"Yeah, but it's affordable and close to work," he replied.

"In this neighborhood, you need to get a better lock on that door." Sue looked out the window. "Not much of a view."

"The landlord said I could install a deadbolt lock as long as I gave him a spare key."

"That's better than nothing. There's no fire escape?" she asked.

"I can always jump out the window. There are nice bushes down there." He laughed. He turned to the door and locked the single doorknob lock and turned to her. "You want to try out the bed?" he asked.

"I thought you would never ask," she purred as she came into his arms and they had a passionate kiss.

Afterward they prepared to leave. It was already four o'clock.

"You want to have supper again with my parents?" she asked.

"I would rather not. Let's find a decent restaurant, maybe that steakhouse we passed in Strongsville?"

"Sounds good to me. How about we go back to the house so I can take a shower and freshen up? Sue asked.

"Sure. I'll do guard duty so your brothers don't try to mess you up."

"Sounds like a plan," she agreed.

CHAPTER 12

Detective Kent was in George Coleman's office at the campus police station. He was giving George details of the autopsy.

"The contents of the victims stomach consisted of what appeared to be either Chinese or Japanese food," he noted. "If we are going to check out restaurants we should focus on those types." He gave a copy of the report to George. "She was definitely raped; we have a sample of semen to verify the DNA sample."

"Ok. There aren't any of those restaurants close to campus; it must be someplace in the city," George replied.

"Yeah, we are working on that. I got a better photo of the girl from her parents. They were pretty upset about their only daughter getting killed this way." He handed a new photo to George. "They both said that their daughter was pretty smart with good street sense. They could not believe she could be taken advantage of so easily," Kent noted.

"The killer must have seemed harmless or she wouldn't have turned her back on him," George replied. "What about the ex-boyfriend?"

"His name is John Ferris. They were pretty serious before they broke up. He has a rock solid alibi. He joined the Merchant Marine and was in a freighter on Lake Superior at the time of the murder. Apparently his joining the Merchant Marine was the reason they broke up," Kent said.

"Well, that doesn't leave us with many leads then," George remarked.

"Do you think our guy is a student?"

"Since he met her in the student union, it is a good possibility," George looked at Kent. "If he is a student then we only have about 3900 suspects to check out." Most of the student body were female nursing students since that was one of the main curriculums of the college. The few men were either in the sports program, the engineering school or the business school.

"Any chance that you keep DNA records of the students?" Kent asked.

"No, that is not a requirement and we have no database for that."

"Well then we should try to eliminate as many of them as possible by checking out if they were on campus or heading home for the break," Kent noted, looking intently at George.

"Yeah, that could be a good idea. We'll start checking that out. Not everyone leaves campus during the break but most of them do since they want to be home with family at Christmas."

"Ok. As your staff looks into that, my guys will be checking restaurants in the city." Kent got up to leave.

"Let's keep in touch." George walked him to the door. After he left, George turned to Andy Hall and asked him to start checking the dorms to see if any men were still on campus. "Just tell them we are making a safety check of the building," he instructed. "Make a list of the men that are still here."

CHAPTER 13

Ron and Sue had stopped sharing supper with the Parker's but instead had elected to go out for dinner, partially because of Sue's step-brothers and because of Mr. Parker's attitude. Mr. Parker had stopped to talk with Ron while he was waiting for Sue to get ready.

"Have you thought about what I told you?" he asked Ron.

"Yes. You may be right, but we are pretty sure we can do this," Ron replied.

"Ok. I hope you are right," he said as he walked away.

"What was that about?" Sue asked as she joined Ron.

"Just warning me that we cannot live apart for four years."

"Come on... lets go," she replied.

Ron was amazed how beautiful she looked with a white blouse, blue skirt and fishnet stockings. She covered it with light brown leather coat unbuttoned in the front. It was a warm night for December, almost 60 degrees but cloudy. Ron was comfortable with just a sports coat over his typical blue shirt and khaki pants. Ron and Sue settled on a meal at a seafood house and then a movie. Then Ron invited her to stop at his apartment for some intimate therapy. She was receptive to the idea so they drove to his new place and parked behind the building. They got out and walked around the hardware store to the street in front to his apartment. It was already dark but the street was illuminated by the street lights in front of the hardware store.

Three Hispanic youths were standing on the sidewalk near his door. They were dressed similarly with worn jeans, light jackets and red bandanas on their heads. They had heard that a new gringo had moved into the neighborhood and had to take his measure. It was important to them that everyone in the neighborhood knew who was boss of the streets. The typical approach was for the leader to stand in front of the man while his two minions started toward the girl and started to caress her. If the man tried to intercede, he would be beaten up. If he let them take the girl then he was already coerced.

"Hey man," the leader approached Ron as his two minions approached Sue. "You the new guy?" He looked at the girl. She was amazingly beautiful he thought. "Hey Chiquita, you want to meet a real man?" he said to Sue.

"You know one?" she asked.

"Very funny..." he said as they walked closer.

"Yeah, we don't want any trouble," Ron answered." You guys don't look Polish."

"Our neighborhood is a few streets away but we control this area," the leader replied.

The two minions approached Sue and started to grab her, which was a mistake. They did not know that she had a 3rd degree black belt in karate. She kicked the first one in the groin and then twirled around and kicked the second one in the throat. (She was aiming for his head but missed). The leader turned to see his two minions lying on the ground writhing in pain. He was very surprised.

"Do you want my girlfriend to beat you up too?" Ron asked. He was prepared to start hitting the leader but the man backed up.

"Wow." The leader was shocked. "I didn't know she was your body guard."

"Shit. I tore my skirt again," she said, looking at her skirt seam.

"Ok Chiquita," The leader backed off, helping his companions to their feet. "We will meet again," he said to Ron.

"We better not," Ron showed him his auxiliary campus police badge. It was too far away for the guy to see it was not a Cleveland Police badge.

"Oh...Ok, I am sorry man," the three limped away down the street. Ron turned to Sue. "You still in the mood?" he asked.

"Why not?" she turned and kissed him. They entered the door to his upstairs apartment. An old man across the street had witnessed the whole thing and was impressed with the newcomer and his girlfriend. Maybe now the thugs would stop harassing the old people in the neighborhood. It was an old neighborhood and most of the Polish youths had grown up and moved away. The neighborhood was gradually becoming a Hispanic ghetto.

CHAPTER 14

It was Christmas day and it had turned colder but had not snowed. The Parker family was off to church. Everyone was wearing their Sunday best clothes but Ron stuck with his blue blazer, white shirt and Khaki pants. He did not wear a tie although Mrs. Parker offered him one from her husband's collection. Sue was dressed in an expensive sleeveless long emerald green cocktail dress with a matching light jacket and a pearl necklace. Mr. Parker had offered for Ron and Sue to ride with them in the large Toyota SUV, but Ron had declined, insisting on driving his Jeep, not wanting to sit too close to the two step brothers. Sue was glad of this. They did agree to sit in the same pew with the family but Ron sat between the step brothers and Sue. The church service was pleasant with a lot of singing of Christmas carols and a short sermon about giving by the pastor. After the service, the pastor was greeting the church goers in the Narthex and saw Sue approach with her family. He greeted Sue warmly, asking how she liked college. She introduced Ron who shook his hand. Sue also showed off her engagement ring which brought a smile to the pastor's face and he wished them well.

Afterward, they all went to a family restaurant in Strongsville that had a special Christmas day buffet style brunch. Every one loaded up their plates and sat down at a table for six. Sue was talking to her mother about the church service. Ron had just sat down next to Sue when step brother Donald who was sitting across from Sue came up carrying a drink and plate of food when he 'tripped' and spilled his large glass of grape juice onto Sue's plate and down the front of her dress. Sue screamed and stood up suddenly knocking her chair backward. Sue's mother looked sternly at the boy.

"I'm sorry, I'm sorry," Donald exclaimed loudly. His brother Damien sitting next to him was smiling quietly.

"That wasn't very nice," Ron stood up looking accusingly at Donald. He saw that Mr. Parker was smiling also.

"My dress is ruined," Sue exclaimed. She looked with hate at the boy.

"Come on, I'll take you home," Ron suggested.

"Let's go." Sue muttered as she grabbed her jacket and headed for the door. People noticed the spreading stain on the front of her dress as she walked toward the exit but she paid no attention.

"I should have expected something like that," Sue said as they neared the Jeep.

"They really hate you, don't they?" Ron opened the door for her.

"No, they just think it's funny," she replied. "One time I had bought a special dress and when I went to take it out of the closet, it was all cut up by someone with a pair of scissors."

"Wow. That is nasty, what did you do?" Ron asked.

"What could I do? They both would have denied doing it," Sue sat in the Jeep. "Another time they put super glue on my chair at dinner. When I went to get up, I was stuck to the chair. I had to undress in front of everyone in order to get off the chair," Sue related.

"I imagine your brothers enjoyed that." Ron started the Jeep and headed back to her house. "How can you keep from hitting them?" he asked.

"In karate we are taught to only use the knowledge we have gained for self-defense," Sue looked at Ron. "Can we go back to the campus today?" She asked.

"I suppose so. I don't start work until next week because of the Christmas holiday shutdown."

"Thank you." She sat the rest of the way in silence.

They got back to the house and Sue went upstairs to pack her bag. She threw the green dress in her trash can as she put on jeans and a sweatshirt. Ron threw his few articles of clothing into his duffle and went down the stairs. The family had not yet returned. Ron had an idea. He went down into the basement. The boy's video game device was on a table in front of the couch facing the wide screen video monitor. He took out his knife and pried open the control box. He used his knife to cut a few wires inside it and closed the box securely. It was a small amount of vengeance but they deserved it.

"Are you ready to go?" she called down to him.

"Yeah, let's hit the road." he replied as he entered from the basement. "Are we taking Joan back also?"

"I texted her but she is staying a couple of more days, so her brother will drive her."

"You're going to miss out on the presents," he said as he looked under the Christmas tree in the great room. A pile of wrapped gifts surrounded the tree..

"That's ok. I never get much anyway. My brothers get a lot of stuff." She took out a small gift for her mother from her purse and put it on the pile.

"I am sorry, but I guess I didn't get you a present in all of the confusion." Ron was not used to giving presents at Christmas. His family was gone a long time ago.

"That's ok. You are my Christmas present." She turned and kissed him passionately.

"Are you sure you want to head back? Classes don't start for another week."

"Yeah, I was glad to visit with my mom but my brothers are terrible," she replied. "I'll text her when we are on the road."

CHAPTER 15

George Coleman was visiting the city police department and was in Detective Kent's office. Kent was just informing him that one of his detectives had found a Japanese Steak House that was apparently where the victim and her murderer had a meal. The waiter remembered the girl but had not paid any attention to her date. Just that he was a slim white man.

"That does not help much," George noted.

"Yeah, sort of a dead end," Kent agreed.

"Do they have video surveillance?"

"No…we struck out there again. We did not get there until four days after the event and they erase their tapes every three days," Kent muttered. "Did you have any luck checking out the men on campus that stayed for the break?"

"Well, we only checked the dormitories, and found 27 total men. Of those, all had alibis except three who said they were sleeping alone in their room," George related. "We brought them in for questioning and asked if they would voluntarily give us DNA samples. They agreed which sort of tells me they weren't involved but I brought the samples with me for analysis anyway," George gave Kent three test tubes containing cotton swabs.

"Ok, we will run these anyway," Kent sighed. "It appears we are at a dead end."

"You got any other ideas?" George asked.

"No, but we will continue to investigate. Maybe take another look at the site where we found her. Maybe we missed something."

"I can check the classes she attended and see who was in those classes. They supposedly met in the Student Union but he may have been attracted to her from class," George replied.

"Yeah, that may be worth a try. Interview her teachers to see if there was anything that stands out as unusual," Kent offered.

"That's a good idea," George agreed. "Maybe I will talk again to her roommate to see if there was anything else she remembers."

CHAPTER 16

Monday

Ron and Sue got back to Campus. They stopped at a grocery store to buy needed supplies for his refrigerator and her small dormitory refrigerator. Afterwards he let Sue off at her dorm and Ron returned to his apartment. He called George Coleman to ask about the investigation.

"Hi George, what's up?" He asked.

"Hello Ron. How was your visit up north?"

"I got to meet Sue's family but we decided to head back early to campus. How is the investigation going?"

"Well, the victim was a student, we confirmed that. Other than we know that they met in the Student Union, we don't have much progress on identifying the murderer," George replied.

"It sounds like he is a student on the campus."

"Yeah, we got his DNA, so if we do get a suspect we can confirm it easily."

"Do you need me to help?" Ron asked. Ron was still a police auxiliary member so he sometimes helped George and the other members of the small campus police force.

"Well, we have run out of leads for now. Once classes are in session next week I will check with the professors of the classes the victim took last semester to see if there are any incidents they remember that may have included her," George related.

"I start work next week at the new job," Ron explained.

"Yeah, if we need you I will call you. You should start your job."

"Ok, thanks," Ron replied.

JANUARY

Ron and Sue spent a quiet New Year's Eve at his apartment, watching the celebration on his TV.

"I have to start work on Monday, so I'll drive up to Cleveland tomorrow," he explained to her.

"Yeah, my first class starts Tuesday morning so I guess we won't see each other until next weekend," she related.

"I want you to be extra cautious with a possible predator roaming campus," he reminded her.

"I think I can take care of myself," she said, reminding him that she did have a third degree black belt in Karate.

"Still, I would feel better if you stayed with a crowd when walking around on campus," he replied. Sue was the most beautiful girl Ron had ever seen so he knew that she would make a desirable target. He did not tell her that the murder victim had the same basic features as Sue. This was probably just a coincidence, he figured.

"Ok," she agreed. She was not worried about being a victim, her karate training had given her a boost of confidence in facing possible confrontations. She was just happy that Ron was concerned for her safety.

CHAPTER 17

*H*e had walked around campus and had located his primary victim. *She had returned to campus. It was too soon to try to get her. He needed another victim as a diversion for the police. So far he had evaded any attention from the police. They were very busy with investigating the first victim but had no idea who they were looking for. He looked like a typical student with no remarkable features that would draw attention. Most people would describe him as general average height and weight and a common face without any identifying marks. He used this as an advantage as it typically allowed him to get close enough to his potential victims without drawing any attention.*

He often shadowed them for several days before making contact. Currently he was interested in three particular girls, all freshmen at the college. Two were nursing students, one was an art student. The colder January weather worked in his favor as he wore a scarf to hide his lower face and a knit hat to hide his hair. He also wore typical blue jeans and a military trench coat he had purchased from an army surplus store. If people wanted to think he was a veteran that was ok with him. He had no real male friends although he did share a dorm room with a roommate named Larry. Larry at first tried to get to know him better but he just replied with short vague answers and kept to himself. After a while Larry ignored him, which was good. Larry was always going out to party with his business student buddies, and had invited him to join them once but was turned down so he did not ask anymore. He did not like Larry; had always been a loner and only been close to his sister. They were similar in many ways but she usually let him do the killing when it was necessary. She was two years older than him but they had been very close. She knew of his appetite for young girls but tolerated it since she had benefitted from his actions in the past. Currently she was doing an assignment for him at his request but thought it was fun. He knew he was in charge of their relationship and wanted to keep it that way. A psychologist would probably describe him as a sociopath but that did not matter to him. He had signed up for the minimum number of credit hours to enable him to stay on campus, but was not interested in grades or getting a degree and typically dropped out of a class after attending a few times. He spent a lot of time at the library using the internet to research his victims. It was amazing what young girls put in their Facebook profiles. It enabled him to know how to approach them and start a conversation. He tried to stay away from girls that had a strong relationship with a boyfriend and concentrated on the ones that were lonely and looking for a relationship. He would appear to be kind and considerate and then when they were comfortably unaware strike them from behind. Although he had a campus dorm room, he had a secret apartment off campus where he would take his victims. He was independently wealthy which he shared with his sister. The wealth allowed him to indulge in his obsession for young, pretty women. He took them out to fancy places or spent money on them so that they were aware that he was financially a good catch for a potential husband. He was, of course, not interested in a permanent relationship.

CHAPTER 18

Ron pulled into the parking lot of the Newmatic Company and parked. It was a cold January day but since it was his first day on the job, he was excited with anticipation. It was snowing lightly but it was not accumulating much. He was dressed in his standard khaki pants and blue button down shirt and blue blazer. There was a side entrance to the building with a row of what looked like revolving doors with bars on them. He tried to walk through but they would not budge. He saw an electric sensor by each door. You would need a special badge to get in this way he thought. He walked around to the front door, entered and stopped at the desk where a security guard was sitting. There was a fence with a gate and the guard was sitting on the other side. An elevator was on the other side of the fenced in area. There was a small opening in the fence where the guard sat at a desk. The guard looked up at him.

"Can I help you?" the guard asked.

"Yes…My name is Ron Pritchard and I am supposed to start work here today," Ron replied.

"You got some identification?"

"Yes…" Ron dug out his driver's license from his wallet and handed it over.

"Hmm… I don't see your name on the list," the guard ran his finger down a list of names. "Oh wait, here it is." The guard saw his name at the bottom of the list. "I gotta call upstairs, you might as well have seat over there," he pointed to a few chairs against the far wall. He did not give back the license. Ron was going to object but decided to merely walk over sit down and wait. After about 15 minutes, the elevator opened and a very beautiful girl in a red pants suit and matching high heeled shoes walked over to the guard. They talked for a minute and the guard handed her Ron's license and pointed at Ron. The girl walked to the gate. The guard pressed a button and the gate opened. The pretty girl approached him. She had long red hair and had perfect makeup. Ron thought she was almost as pretty as Sue. He stood up.

"You are Ron Pritchard?" she asked smiling.

"Yes…" he was stunned by her beauty close up.

"Hello. My name is Penelope Webber, but you can call me Penny." She motioned for him to follow her. He noticed that she had a very pleasing perfume scent and her figure was perfect.

They walked to the elevator as the guard closed the gate. They got into the elevator and she pushed the button for three. As the doors closed she turned to him and appraised his appearance. "You are a lot more handsome than I expected," she purred since they were alone in the elevator. "I figured you would be a nerdy engineer type." She smiled at him with her perfect teeth.

"Ahh…" he started to say something but was at a loss for words.

"Don't worry…you and I will get along just fine," she replied.

The door opened into a hallway. There were offices with windows on the wide hallway. She led him down to a room with several people in it. It was the Human Resources office. Penny led him into a side office where an older gray-haired woman wearing a grey pants suit was sitting. Penney bent down to whisper something in the woman's ear and handed her Ron's driver's license. Then Penny turned and walked out of the office. As she passed Ron she said, "See you later," in a sexy low voice.

"Mr. Pritchard?" the older woman asked. "My name is Gerta, please sit down."

"Yes," he sat in the chair facing her.

"I see by your records that you are just out of college. Your grade point average is very high. You must have impressed someone quite a bit since I did not see a transcript of your resume or job application." She looked at him with a stern look.

"Yes I was an intern here last year and Mr. Tyler offered me job," Ron replied. Jeff Tyler was one of the engineering managers.

"Yes…I see that. Well, we have some paperwork to go over and I need you to go next door and get a photo for your employee badge." Ron wondered why the badge he had used previously last year was not available but he obediently did what she asked. After a while all of the paperwork was done and he had a new badge. It was a different color than the one he had last year. Gerta called someone on the phone and returned his driver's license. A minute later Penny entered and told him she was taking him up to the fourth floor for Engineering to Jeff Tyler's office.

"I know where his office is, I can find it," Ron protested, but she lead him to the elevator anyway.

"That's ok, I work in Engineering too." She smiled at him again. He was on the point of telling her that he was already engaged, but for some reason he didn't. She led him to Jeff Tyler's office and then turned to walk away. Jeff looked up from his computer and saw Ron.

"Well, you finally showed up," he exclaimed, smiling. "I see you were escorted here by the ice maiden."

"Penny? She seemed pretty nice to me." Ron replied.

"Really? Oh well, anyway you are here." Jeff noted. "I have a special assignment for you." Ron was eager to get back to the design work. He really liked making drawings of the component parts last year.

"I know you would like to get back in the design group again but I have a pressing problem in the test lab and I'm hoping you can solve some problems for us," Jeff explained. "So, I am assigning you to the test lab as a test engineer."

Ron was shocked. He really thought he would be working with the design group. He had made a lot of friends there last year and they had accepted him as an equal.

"But I thought I did good in the design group," Ron protested.

"You did. But I need someone to go in the test lab and help out. It might be temporary. You could be back here in a few months," Jeff explained. Just then an older man in his fifties looked in. He was heavyset and wore a gray three piece suit with a blue tie.

"Is this our new test engineer?" the man walked up to Ron and shook his hand.

"Ahh… Hi Lou. This is Ron Pritchard our new engineer. Ron, this is Lou Roberts, our vice president." Jeff made the introductions.

Ron stood up. "Very happy to meet you sir," Ron addressed the vice president.

"We sure could use your help in the lab. We are way behind the qualification schedule for those actuators," Lou said. "According to Jeff here, you are the right man for the job." He turned away and walked out.

Ron looked at Jeff and now understood why he was going to the test lab. Jeff looked at Ron with sad eyes. "Sorry about this, but I have no choice," Jeff apologized.

"That's ok. I always like a challenge," Ron replied. "Where is the test lab?" he asked.

"It's up the hill, past the railroad tracks. You can't miss it. It's the tallest building up there, right next to the manufacturing plant," Jeff informed him.

CHAPTER 19

S ue Conner was only taking four courses this semester, two art classes, Chemistry and Math 101. She really liked the art classes; the instructors were very knowledgeable and friendly. The art classes were sort of small, only 12 in one and 16 in the other. That let her get a lot of personal instruction and she really liked that. The math class was huge with about 90 kids in a slanted auditorium setting. Apparently all freshmen had to take this class as a requirement so they lumped them together in one big room. The instructor was apparently bored teaching freshman math and had a graduate assistant do most of the teaching. Sue tried her best to follow along but math was not one of her favorite subjects. She had passed it in high school but did not take the advanced courses, so a lot of what this class was about was new to her. A typical straight A student, she figured she would be lucky to get a C in this class. At least her friend Joan was in the same class so she could try to work with her to understand the algebra terms.

Chemistry was even worse than math. She was in a room with about 30 other students and the instructor was apparently of Indian heritage and he spoke with a heavy accent that she could not understand easily. Luckily he put most of what he was lecturing on a blackboard behind him. She had not taken chemistry in high school either so all of what the professor was showing about electron levels was totally foreign to her. She looked around and everyone else appeared to be following along, taking notes and paying rapt attention. She started taking notes also but none of it made any sense to her. What the heck was Avogadro's number anyway? Different electron levels and ionic and covalent bonds were all new to her. She had purchased the thick book for the class and hoped she could read it later and hope it made some sense. If she was going to be an art teacher, why did she need this course? she wondered. At the end of the day, she was exhausted. It was late afternoon and she started to walk back to her dormitory. It was cold but she had a thick coat on so she was pretty warm. There was a slight ground covering of snow but someone had salted the walkway so it was pretty much clear. She wondered if Joan would want to walk over to one of the on campus restaurants or just cook something in their room. She felt funny, as if someone was watching her. She stopped and looked around but did not see anyone. Just getting paranoid she thought. It was already starting to get dark and she had to walk about a half mile to get to her dorm. As she progressed she felt it again. Someone must be following her but in the dark she could not see anyone. She walked closer to the street lights along the pathway and saw a figure up ahead just standing there. As she got closer she saw he was wearing a police uniform. It was Andy Hall, one of Ron's police friends.

"Hello Andy," she said walking up to him.

"Why are you out here in the dark alone?" he asked.

"My chemistry class is way over in Drake Hall so I have to walk this way to get back to my dorm, she explained.

"You have class on Tuesday and Thursdays?" he asked.

"Yes. But it's not that far to walk. If it was summer I might take a bike but it doesn't ride well in the snow," she replied.

"Ok, but from now on I will meet you at Drake Hall and escort you home." Andy said.

"Oh, you don't have to do that." Sue looked back at the way she came.

"No. It's Ok. George wants me to patrol the campus to prevent any young girls from being attacked. Since you are engaged to one our guys, it is only fitting that I make sure you are safe." Andy was smiling.

"Well, ok then. I appreciate the escort." She was tempted to tell him that she thought she was being followed but he would just think she was being paranoid. Ever since the news broke about the girl getting killed on campus, all of the women at the college were nervous and trying to be extra cautious. Joan hardly left the dorm when it was dark out. And it got dark really early in January. Andy and Sue walked away chatting cheerfully.

He had watched her from the bushes along the walkway. He had almost snuck up on her when she ran into the cop. Oh well, he would try again some other time. He had other targets to choose from. He turned away frustrated. He was getting the itch again. He would have to find another victim soon. He would look up the nursing student next.

CHAPTER 20

Ron walked up the hill from the four story office building and crossed the railroad tracks. The test area and manufacturing plant was to the right of the road. A huge parking lot was on the left side and was packed with parked cars. There was a guard shack next to a fence gate. The gate was open so Ron walked through to the guard house and showed the guard his badge.

"How do I get to the test lab?" Ron asked.

"Well, you could go up to that second man door next to the large overhead door, but they typically keep it locked. So… you need to go through the first man door before the large overhead door. Be sure to swipe your card on the card reader," the guard instructed. The building was large, at least three stories high. He walked to the door and swiped his badge. There was a magnetic strip on the back that was similar to a credit card that triggered an electric lock to open. The door opened and he walked in. Immediately he was bombarded by the sounds of machines and people shouting and tow motors moving about. He looked around to see if he could find a manager or supervisor. He finally saw a man in a white shirt and tie with a clipboard directing a couple of men moving a large fixture.

"Excuse me…can you direct me to the test lab?" he asked the man.

"Yes?" the man turned his attention to him. He had ear protectors on so did not hear what Ron said.

"I said, can you direct me to the test lab?" Ron repeated.

"Oh. You must be the new guy. You see that far wall?" he pointed to an area with another large overhead door and a man door next to it, about fifty yards away. "Go in there, turn to your right until you see the test office." He smiled at him.

"Thanks," Ron replied.

"Good luck. You'll need it," the man replied as he turned back to his workers.

Ron wondered what he meant by that. He walked toward the door. The overhead door was up so he just walked through and turned to his right. There were three test towers he walked by but he did not see any tests going on. He continued to walk and came to an open area with a lot of skids with parts on them. Next to this was a brightly lit office. Four people were sitting at desks, apparently busy with schematics or writing in their computers. Two were older men probably in their fifties, a young guy looking at an electrical schematic and another guy who was busy trying to fix a part. There was an enclosed office in the back with an older bald headed man sitting at a desk reading a document. He opened the door and saw the young guy in a near desk sketching out something on an electrical circuit.

"Hello, can you tell me where Harvey Johnson is?" Ron asked the young man.

"Yeah...in there." He pointed to the back office. He was not smiling, apparently upset because someone interrupted him.

Ron walked up to the small office and knocked on the door. Harvey motioned him to come in.

"Hello. You must be Ron?" the old guy got up and shook his hand. "Sit down, sit down." He motioned to a chair.

"Yes I'm Ron Pritchard, your new test engineer." Ron sat down.

"Well, we'll see about that. The previous guy only lasted four months," Harvey noted.

"Really? What happened to him?" Ron asked.

"Never mind about that. What type of test background do you have?" Harvey asked.

"Ahh…well I just got out of college. I'm afraid I don't have much experience," Ron answered.

Harvey groaned. "Why do they send me these guys?" He looked up at the ceiling.

"Look. I can do it, I'm a fast learner." Ron begged. "I was supposed to be in the design group but they said that help was needed in the test area."

"Ok. We'll give you a chance. We have a very difficult qualification problem and maybe someone with a fresh outlook will be able to do it," Harvey said doubtfully. Let me introduce you to the troops. He led Ron out into the outer office.

"Attention everybody. We have a new engineer to work with us." Harvey began to introduce them. "The man in the white shirt and black tie is Stan Welland, our lead engineer. The fellow with the jeans and gray sport coat is Bob Valley, a senior engineer. The young fellow at the left is one of our instrument technicians, Rick Nemi. And the other guy over there is Gary Ault, another instrument technician. This is Ron Pritchard, a new engineer, fresh out of college."

Harvey smiled. "Stan, please assign him a desk and have him start on the actuator qualification." Harvey turned and went back into his office.

"So…You are a college boy huh?" Stan sneered at him. None of the test people had college degrees but had worked their way up from lowly entrance level employees over a period of years.

"Ahh… yes, just graduated last month." Ron answered.

"That's great," Stan turned to Bob Valley and they both started to laugh. The technicians didn't laugh but looked at Ron with sad eyes.

"Well. I'll give you this desk over here. The last guy that used it didn't stick around very long." He pointed to a desk in front of Gary Ault. "There should still be some office supplies in the drawers."

"Thanks," Ron replied, moving over and sitting down. He felt like a total outsider in here but realized that he just had to be successful here or he was going to lose his job.

"Here's your assignment." Stan thew a bunch of thick specifications on top of his desk. "You are already three months late so you better get cracking." Stan sneered at him again.

Ron started to look at the specifications and saw that it was for two large hydraulic actuators. At least he was familiar with the actuator concept, he had studied them in hydraulics class. As he started to read through the document a tall man in a black suit walked in. He had a black mustache and black hair. He walked up to Stan.

"You got my actuators tested yet?" he asked Stan.

"There's your boy," Stan pointed at Ron.

"You're new, aren't you?" The tall man turned to Ron.

"Yes. Just started today." Ron answered.

"Well, I am Bill Hobb, the airframe customer representative," the tall man replied. "Can you qualify those actuators for me?" he said pointing to the specifications on Ron's desk.

"Yes sir, but I haven't had time to read these documents yet," Ron replied. (He heard Stan and Bob laugh behind him).

"Well, I hope you can…everyone else here says it can't be done and they want us to change the specs." He looked with malice at the two senior test engineers who suddenly were very busy with their paperwork.

Ron looked at the man. "I will give it my best effort." Ron said smiling.

"I hope you are good to your word. You are already three months late." Mr. Hobb turned and walked out of the room.

Stan looked at the new guy. This kid was a young wet-nosed college weenie with no test experience. He was bound to fail. Stan had already looked at trying to do the temperature shock test but it was impossible. The actuator had to be taken out of the oven at 250 degrees F while extending and retracting with 3000 psi of hydraulic pressure and plunged into a minus 60 degrees F cold chamber in 5 seconds. Then it had to be done in reverse, cold temperature to hot temperature. While this was being done, all of the temperatures and pressures had to be recorded for a report. It just could not be done. The furnace oven and the cooler were forty feet apart and there was no way to do it in this lab. The hydraulic test stand could give you 3000 psi but it was even farther from the oven. This new kid was going to give up and leave soon just like the first guy that tried it. Stan smiled to himself. The kid had promised Hobb he could do it without even reading the spec. The new kid was going to be a short timer for sure. He smiled to himself. He didn't want any new guy to threaten his position of chief engineer. He and Bob Valley had worked together for almost 15 years and had found a good symbiotic relationship as they covered each other's asses. Harvey, the lab manager was approaching retirement and Stan knew he was the obvious replacement.

CHAPTER 21

George Coleman was in his police office talking to Detective Kent. He looked very disappointed. "I've interviewed all of the victim's professors from last semester but none of them remembered anything unusual," he related to Kent.

"Yeah, we've had no luck at our end either, every possible lead was a dead end," Kent related.

"So… what do we do now? Wait for him to strike again?" George asked.

"I hate to admit it but this guy may have fooled us. We are still going to work it… but we have no leads at the moment." Kent sighed. "We still have no matches for his DNA – even the FBI files did not contain it."

"We never did find her purse or her cell phone. I asked her roommate to call the cell phone but it must be turned off or destroyed." George said.

"Yeah, He is probably too smart not to have destroyed her cell phone. How about her Facebook account… were there any threats or strange posts?" Kent asked.

"Her roommate showed me her internet accounts, I didn't see anything threatening."

"Well then, I guess we are out of options. I still want to have my guys look at her internet accounts – maybe they will see something you missed."

"Yeah, that's a good idea. I wasn't trained to be a profiler," George agreed.

"What a shame… She was such a young pretty girl and he used her and threw her away like a piece of trash." Kent got up and walked to the door. "Let's keep in touch."

"If I find any clues I will let you know at once." George agreed.

Andy Hall came over and sat next to George. "Do they have any leads?" he asked as Kent walked out of the campus police station.

"No…everything is a dead end." George said, frustrated. "Just keep patrolling around the campus. Maybe an increased police presence will throw this guy off."

"We need more guys," Andy stated.

"I know but we don't have the budget."

"I wish Ron was here to help out. He's pretty smart." Andy noted.

"Yeah, but he has his own life and that is about working as an engineer up in Cleveland."

"I know." Andy replied.

CHAPTER 22

S ue was sitting next to Joan in math class. Class was just over so they got up together and headed for the exit.

"Oh look. Isn't that Beth Mentor?" Joan exclaimed. "She was in our class at school. Look, she is talking to Greg Sommers. He's that guy you dated in high school a couple of times!" Joan remarked as she and Sue walked over to them.

"Wow, this is like a high school reunion," said Beth as Joan and Sue approached them.

"Hello," Sue said to Beth. "I didn't know you were at this college. Hi Greg." Sue was more interested in Beth than Greg since her previous dates with him in high school were uncomfortable. All he really wanted was to lure her into a sexual encounter.

"Yeah, this is supposed to be one of the top schools for nursing," Beth responded. "What are you going for?" she asked Sue.

"Well, I'm an Art major, hope to become a teacher," Sue said as they hugged.

"How are you doing, Greg?" Joan asked him.

"I'm ok...going for a business degree," he said, smiling at Joan and Sue.

"Hard to imagine all of us here from South High," Beth noted.

"Yeah...small world, isn't it," Greg replied. "Got to go. See you guys later," Greg said as he walked to the exit.

"I was just talking to Greg about the math class…I think he wants to ask me out," Beth giggled.

"I am warning you…He tends to be somewhat aggressive," Sue replied.

"Yeah, it seems like it. What do you think of math class?" Beth asked.

"Well, it is a requirement but I don't know why I have to take it when I am an Art major," Sue replied. The girls remained and chatted for a while, discussing their class schedules and the college life in general. Sue showed Beth her engagement ring and they had to talk about that for a few minutes. Later Sue and Joan walked to their dorm.

"I noticed you didn't say much to Greg," Joan noted.

"Yeah, I know he is someone from our old high school, but we never really got along that well," Sue told her. "He was only interested in going to bed with a girl, any girl for that matter."

"Yeah, he even approached me once but I was dating someone else at the time," Joan laughed.

"Do you want to stop at the student union to grab a snack before the next class?" Sue asked her.

"Sounds good to me," Joan agreed.

CHAPTER 23

*H*e *was sitting three tables away from her. The Student Union was crowded and noisy. She was talking to her friend. He had been tracking her for days now but she was totally unaware. He had learned her name from her notebook that she left open when she went to the ladies' room in the library. After a thorough internet and Facebook search he found enough information about her to almost know her intimately. It was too crowded in here now to do anything. He could not afford a scene if she reacted wrongly. He would bide his time. She was, he thought, perfect. Well mannered, attractive and well dressed. She was a brunette with green eyes, a feature that he could not resist. Her friend got up and left. He decided to try anyway. He stood up and walked toward her. She was looking at a book he recognized as a biology text. He pretended to bump her chair as he walked by and turned to say excuse me.*

"Excuse me, I am so sorry... Hey, are you Barbara Perry from Harvey High?" he asked

"Yes. Do I know you?" she replied.

"Oh, you probably don't remember me, we were in the same civics class with Mr. Howard." (He had never been to Harvey High but she had written about it a lot in her internet entries.)

"Really?" she looked at him closer. "Yes, you were in that class?"

"Yeah...I remember you gave a presentation on women's rights. I still remember it," he lied.

"Wow. I think I do remember you...did you sit at the back of the class?" she asked.

"Yeah, that was me." He saw that her girlfriend was coming back. "Hey, I got to rush off; maybe see you again sometime?"

"Sure," she smiled. "What was your name..." she asked but he had already walked away.

"Who was that?" her girlfriend said, sitting down. She had gotten them each a hot chocolate drink.

"Ahh... just someone from Harvey High."

"Really? He didn't look familiar to me," her friend said.

"Well, I didn't get his name, he had to rush off. Maybe I'll see him again."

"He must have graduated a year ahead of us," her friend figured.

"Yeah, that must be it." The civics class was a mix of sophomore and junior students so that was possible. It was a small world, she thought.

CHAPTER 24

Ron was reading the specification on the actuators. The previous engineer had done some of the testing but the temperature shock test was never done. He re-reviewed the spec again. He had an idea of how to do it but it would take a lot of equipment. Stan and Rick left the office to start setting up a test in the static frame on different components for the same aircraft program as the actuators. Bob Valley left to go outside to smoke a thin cigar. That left Ron and Gary Ault in the office. Harvey Johnsen was in his office, sleeping upright with a paper in his hand.

Ron went out and looked at the actuators he was supposed to test. They both were about a foot long with a ten inch stroke. They were slightly different since they were used in different locations on the aircraft. They both used the same hydraulic oil type, so could be in the same test setup. Ron returned to the office and sat down at his desk.

"Welcome to the test lab." Gary said from behind.

"Thanks," Ron turned to look at him. Gary was a middle aged guy wearing a blue T-shirt and blue jeans, but he was smiling at Ron. "How come everyone here is so unfriendly?" Ron asked.

"Well, you are a new guy and a threat to the test engineers," Gary responded.

"How come you are different?"

"I'm in the same boat as you. I am new also. They just won't let me do any instrumentation…they make Rick do everything. They made me spend a month just making an inventory of all the test equipment instead of what I was hired to do," Gary explained.

"So…you have a list of test equipment?" Ron asked.

"Yes, you need to see it?"

"Please, I have an idea how to do this test but I don't know what equipment is available." Ron asked.

"Here it is," Gary handed four typewritten pages of equipment. "If you want some help, I can help you."

"That would be great," Ron replied as he scanned the list." What are these heater/cooler units you have here?" He pointed to an entry on page 2.

"Yeah, those are very old, but they might still work. You want to see them?" Gary asked.

"Can you show me?"

"Come on, I found them in the storage room out back. I bet no one knows they are even in there," Gary replied. They went out back and Gary showed him the units. The long rectangular box units each had a 5000 watt electric heater and a strange looking slanted tube device with holes in it attached to a long handled valve. A couple of old empty liquid nitrogen tanks were also in the back. Gary explained that he thought the connector to the cooling unit fit the connecting pipes on the tall liquid nitrogen bottles. Apparently you connected the valve fitting to the nitrogen bottles with the metal hose and regulated the flow of liquid nitrogen into the device with the long handled valve. The holes in the slanted tube would squirt the liquid nitrogen as it turned to gas and cooled the chamber. The heater/cooler units had six-inch diameter holes at each end so a duct could be attached. If you hooked up a fan to the box you could move the hot or cold air to where you wanted it.

"This is perfect," Ron said. "I know how we can do the test. You want to help me?"

"It's better than sitting in the office doing nothing," Gary replied.

"Does this company have a carpenter shop?"

"I believe so. They made some holding fixtures for Stan a few weeks ago," Gary smiled.

"Ok, I am going to make a couple sketches of what I want. Can you look at that temperature shock test spec and figure out what instrumentation we need?" Ron asked.

"That sounds good. I was hoping to do some actual instrumentation work," Gary smiled at him again, eager to get started.

Ron returned to the office and started sketching up a schematic of what he wanted to do. Bob Valley saw he was at work designing something but was not curious enough to look. Ron took his sketch and showed it to his new boss, Harvey.

"You think this will work?" Harvey Johnsen asked, looking at the sketch.

"Yes it will, but I need your signature to get the carpenter shop to build it," Ron exclaimed.

"Well, ok then, I guess it's worth a try." He signed the paper work order. He did not think it would work but the kid wanted to try it. Why not give him enough rope to hang himself he figured. At least he had an idea. Nobody else had even tried to do this test.

CHAPTER 25

S ue had walked over to Ron's apartment. She was waiting for Ron to come home. She was wearing blue Jeans and a heavy down jacket since it was getting colder at night. It was late Friday but she couldn't wait to see him. Since it was cold outside she knocked on his landlord's door.

"Hello Sue," Matt greeted her at the door." You waiting for Ron?" he asked.

"Yes, it's almost eight o'clock and I figured he might be coming home soon."

"Well come on in, it's too cold to wait outside," Matt replied.

"Hi Sue," Becky greeted her. "How are your classes this semester?"

"The art and math classes are ok, but I am struggling with chemistry," Sue complained.

"Well come in and sit down," Becky said. "Ron should be here in a while; he only works to five right?"

"I think so. I am not sure."

"Did you walk here by yourself? It's not safe to be out at night by yourself," Becky alluded to the killer on campus.

"I did think I was being followed, but every time I turned to look no one was there. Just must be nerves, I guess," Sue replied. Just then they heard Ron's Jeep pull in the drive way. "Here he is now!" Sue jumped up and ran to the door.

"Have a good night," Matt said as she went outside.

"Thanks," Sue replied as she closed the door.

"Hey…how are you?" Ron greeted Sue as he exited the Jeep.

"About time…" Sue said as she leaped into his arms, kissing him.

"Wow! Did you miss me?" Ron asked.

"You have been gone for a whole week. What do you think?" she replied.

"Ok. I stayed a little bit late, sorry. The traffic out of Cleveland was really bad. I'm going to start leaving a little early on Fridays so I will miss the traffic."

"Did you eat yet?" she asked.

"No… do you want to go down to the diner down the street?"

"Sure…I only had a snack at the dorm before I walked here," she said.

"Oh, Ok, let's go." It was only a short walk of about two blocks. "You walked over here from campus?" he asked.

"Yes, it's only about eight blocks. I wanted to see you," she replied.

"It's probably too dangerous to be out at night by yourself."

"You forget I have a third degree black belt?"

"Yeah, but I would feel better if you stayed at the dorm…and I will drive over there from now on and not stop here first," he implored.

"Ok. That will work," she agreed.

They entered the small diner and sat in a booth. They both ordered cheeseburgers and Cokes. He also ordered French fries.

"So how is the new job?" she asked.

"Well, they transferred me to the test lab since they are shorthanded for this qualification testing," he answered. "How are your classes?" he asked

"Art and math are ok, but I am lost in chemistry class. I need some personal tutoring."

"Maybe I can help you. I got a 'B' in chemistry," he replied.

Later they walked back to his apartment. He had turned the heat down since he was gone most of the week. He turned up the thermostat and they sat on his couch to watch TV. She cuddled up to him and they started necking which led to some personal intimate chemistry in his bedroom. Then he drove her back to the campus. They made plans to go to the library the next day so he could help her study.

CHAPTER 26

JANUARY

He had discretely followed her from a distance. When she had turned to look behind her, he had ducked to the side. He was closing in on her when she turned into a driveway and knocked on the door of the house. Maybe she saw him? He crossed the street and walked slowly by the house. Then he saw the red Jeep drive up and pull into the driveway. It must be the boyfriend, he thought. She came out and greeted the boyfriend. He figured he would not get to her tonight. He turned around and headed back towards the campus. He still had two other girls he was tracking. The other two would be easier to approach anyway. He got back to his dorm and hid his "stinger" and gray tape in his closet. He was lucky in his choice of dorm rooms. He had ditched the roommate and changed dorms. It was a single so he did not have a roommate. He had paid the building manager a hundred dollars for the assignment of the single room in the Sanford building, explaining that he needed a quiet room to study. He was signed up for classes but was not really concerned for the grades. He got on his computer and started to review the Facebook pages of the other two girls he had hacked into. Both girls tended to communicate with their friends about their classes and people they met and what activities they had planned. It was just too easy, he thought. He almost knew as much about them as their friends.

CHAPTER 27

Ron was setting up his test of the actuators with Gary Ault's help. The two senior test engineers, Stan Welland and Bob Valley stayed as far away from the setup as possible. They did not want to be associated with the obvious upcoming failure of the test. Ron did not mind. He had briefed both Bill Hobb (the airframe representative) and Tom Noga (the government inspector) of the test and showed them how he was going to perform the test using a transfer box between the cold and hot chambers. They were both skeptical but they admitted it might work. Later Ron was at his desk working on the paperwork for the test.

"Hello Ron." Penny came into the office and walked over to him. She was wearing a sexy red miniskirt, red high heel shoes and a tight white blouse that emphasized her ample bosom. She had her coat over her arm but handed him an envelope.

"Oh…Hi Penny." Ron was startled by her obvious beauty.

"I brought you your paycheck. Since you aren't in the system yet for automatic deposits I thought I would deliver it in person," she purred, smiling at him.

"Thank you," he replied accepting the check, "You didn't have to make a special trip, I could have walked down the hill."

"No problem. I needed a break away from my desk anyway." She smiled at him. Stan and Bob looked at her with awe. Even Gary and

Rick were amazed at seeing her be friendly with someone. She was known throughout the company as the 'Ice Maiden' since she was all professional and had rejected all attempts by all of the men to get to know her.

"Well...I appreciate it." Ron smiled back at her.

"See you around," she smiled at him again and walked sexily out of the office.

Stan and Bob looked at each other in amazement. Penny would not even say hello to them when they passed her in the hallway. What did the new guy have that she was so attracted to? Rick and Gary looked at each other with a puzzled look on their faces also.

Gary waited until she was out of sight and asked Ron "How come she likes you?" he asked.

"What do you mean? She seems very warm and friendly," Ron replied.

"Only to you, it seems," Gary smiled.

"I doubt that," Ron turned away and looked at the check. Wow! It was more money than he had ever had at one time. He had set the test time for tomorrow morning. He just hoped it would work as he planned. He had Gary go and check the instrumentation and recording device one last time.

"Everything is ready," he announced to Ron.

"Well, I am coming in early to get everything running," he told Gary. "It should take a couple of hours for the temperature to stabilize."

"Do you need me here early?" Gary asked.

"No... just come in at your regular time but be prepared to start the instrumentation when you first get here." Ron had made sure that the two witnesses would be available for the test.

"Ok. No problem." Gary was relieved that he didn't need to be early.

CHAPTER 28

*H*e was in the student union again. He expected to see Barbara but she was not at any of the tables. So, he opened his text book and pretended to study the boring subject matter. Then he saw Barbara enter and head to a table with a girlfriend. She was nicely dressed wearing tan slacks and a frilly blue blouse. She put down her books and coat and looked up and saw him sitting there about three tables away by himself. She said something to her friend and then walked over to his table.

"Frank?" she asked as she sat down next to him. "It is Frank, isn't it?"

"Yes…Hello," he said, acting surprised to see her.

"You're Barbara, right?" he inquired.

"Yes. I'm sorry to bother you but you said we had a class together at Harvey High."

"Yes. I believe you were one of the sophomores, I was a junior that year," he recalled a paragraph in her Facebook account where she mentioned meeting a boy from Harvey High.

"Well, I just wanted to say hello. I don't see that many people from our old high school." She acted embarrassed.

"That's ok. I was hoping to run into you again, maybe ask you out for date," he said lightly. He did not want to scare her, but she had approached him so he gambled that she might be receptive. "That is, unless you are going steady with someone." He looked into her beautiful green eyes and smiled.

"Oh…no…I am not going steady with anyone right now…" she hesitated. "Yes, I would like to go out with you." Her face flushed red.

"Why don't you give me your number and I will call you later? I have to go to class right now." He stood up.

"OK, here it is." She wrote down her number on a page from her notebook, tore it out and handed it to hm.

"Ok. I'll see you later," he replied, placing the paper in his pocket and turning away. Wow! he thought as he walked out the door. This was a lot easier than I thought it would be. He would wait a couple of days and then call her to go out for dinner and a movie. She would be waiting for his call but did not want her to think he was too eager. Better to keep her waiting and wanting him to call. She would then be a lot more receptive. He could not wait to get back to his dorm room to see what she wrote on her Facebook page about him.

CHAPTER 29

Ron had the test all set up. Gary had inspected all of the instrumentation and said he was ready. Ron called the inspectors and asked them to come to the test lab. He had warned them the day before that he would run the test this morning so they did not schedule anything else today. When Bill Hobb and Tom Noga arrived, he had them review all of the thermocouple readouts showing the temperatures in the two adjacent boxes. They looked through the clear plexiglas window and could see the test unit. He motioned for Gary to start the data recording device and started the pressurization of the unit. As it started to extend and retract, he pushed the sliding platform from one chamber to the other, as it continued cycling back and forth from retract to extend. The inspectors noted that the pressure was 3000 psig as per the specification and that temperature of the unit started to change from minus 60 degrees to the 250 degrees. The transition from one temperature to the other was in one second (the specification allowed 5 seconds). The test was a success.

"Well, you did it." Bill Hobb came over to Ron when the test was over. "I am impressed."

Tom Noga walked up to him, smiled and said "Good job," which was unusual for him since he was known to be a real stickler for test procedures and results.

"It was simple, I figured out how to do it the first day I was here, but I couldn't have done it without Gary," he pointed to the instrumentation guy. "He was the one that made it happen."

"Good job, Gary," Bill Hobb went over to shake Gary's hand. "We appreciate your effort here."

"Ahh...thanks," Gary said. He was amazed that Ron was giving him credit for the test. It was the first time anyone in the test lab had shared credit with him.

Ron had the inspectors sign the test data sheets and noted that he would get them a copy of his test report in a day or two.

Bill Hobb walked into the test office and knocked on Harvey's door, waking him from his mid- morning nap.

"Yes?" Havey asked as Bill entered the office.

"Your new engineer just qualified the actuator," Bill replied. "He is a good one."

"Really?" Harvey was surprised. Both of his senior test engineers, Stan and Bob had said that the specified test was too unrealistic, even if it did simulate what happened on the actual aircraft. They had both petitioned to get the specification changed.

"Well, your new guy did a great job," Bill noted, as he turned to leave.

"Thank you," Harvey smiled. Bill had been pestering him for over three months to finish the actuator qualification and the new kid had done the impossible with his first try. He would have to give this kid some closer attention.

Stan and Bob could not believe that the funny setup the kid built actually worked. They now realized that he was a real threat to them.

That afternoon Bill Hobb visited the engineering fourth floor office of Lou Roberts. Penny, Lou's executive secretary looked up from her computer.

"Yes?" she asked him. She knew he was the important airframe representative but was not going to change her demeaner just because he was important.

"Look Honey, can I see Lou for a minute?" Bill smiled at her.

"I will check," she said icily, not smiling at his attempt to be friendly. She walked to Lou's door and looked in. "A Mr. Hobb to see you?"

"Sure, send him in." Lou looked up as Bill entered his office. "Sit down, Bill," he motioned to an empty chair. Bill had been pestering him about the poor performance of his test lab and he dreaded seeing him again. "What can I do for you?" he asked.

"I just wanted to inform you that that new engineer you put in the test lab is a real firecracker." He used his southern drawl. (He grew up in South Carolina). "He just qualified my actuators this morning. Why didn't you send him up there sooner?"

"The new kid…" Lou searched his memory for the boy's name.

"Yeah, Ron Pritchard. He and that Gary guy did a super job in only a couple of weeks."

"Well, he is a new hire…he just finished college," Lou remembered.

"He can run one of my programs any time. He is the best engineer I have seen here." Bill replied, exaggerating somewhat. "I think he has a good future at your company."

Penny had stood by the door eavesdropping but out of sight. Wow… she thought. That Ron guy must be a good engineer or he wouldn't be getting this praise. As Bill and Lou finished their conversation, Penny slipped back into her seat.

"You know, it wouldn't hurt you to smile once in a while," Bill paused at her desk. He thought she was the most attractive secretary he had ever seen.

She turned to look at him. "I do when I have a reason to," she responded as she went back to her work.

"Right." Bill walked out into the hall. She is an Ice Maiden, he thought to himself. He wondered what it would take to crack her armor. Oh well, he was a lot older than she was and obviously was not attracted to him, he thought. Too bad, he would have liked to have gotten close to her.

CHAPTER 30

*H*e finally called Barbara. He asked if she would like to go out for dinner and a movie. She was so happy to finally hear from him that she said yes. They went out to eat at a fancy Italian restaurant and then attended a new movie that the critics were raving about. Barbara was impressed that he did not even make a pass at her or offer to kiss her at the end of the date. Instead, he meekly offered that he had really enjoyed sharing the time with her and hoped that she would consider going out with him again. She readily agreed and they made plans for the next Saturday night. (He had read in her Facebook entry that she was hoping that he would not be very aggressive, at least not on the first date). She had been impressed the way he rushed to open a door for her and listened so intently during dinner as if he really cared about her. He figured that it made him out to be a gentleman…something he definitely was not… but he could act the part. He doubted that she would enjoy the actual plans he had for her on Saturday. He had called his sister to see how things were going at her end. She reported that the new job was easy and she was making good progress on his request.

CHAPTER 31

George Coleman parked his police cruiser by the Student Union and walked toward the forested area behind the building. He had patrolled this area periodically ever since the murdered young girl had been found there. It was heavily overcast this morning. It had snowed last night and an accumulated 3 inches covered the ground. It was quiet for a Sunday morning and he did not see many students on the campus. At least it was not windy, he thought as he pushed up the collar on his coat to try to hold out the cold. It must be about 10 degrees this morning, he thought. He had ordered new coats for his deputies but they had not arrived yet. The old jackets were ok for the fall weather but not quite adequate for the winter weather. He was thinking of this when he entered the trees and walked to the spot where the poor girl had lain. He got to the tree. Everything looked normal. A few feet away was a snow-covered figure on the ground. Oh no! he thought… It can't be happening again. He bent over the figure and brushed off the snow. It was a young girl, totally naked, lying face down. He felt for a pulse but there was none. She was dead. He stood back. He ran to his police car and called the city police and informed them what he had found. He had hoped that the first victim was a one-time occurrence, but now it seemed that it could be a serial killer. He went back to his car and sat in it waiting for the city police and their forensic team to show up. It only took about fifteen minutes. He got out of the car and directed them to the body. Detective Kent also arrived and walked to the scene. He saw George standing there watching as the forensic people did their thing.

"So…it looks like we have another one?" he asked George.

"Yeah, I guess so." George looked down at the ground. "I was hoping this wouldn't happen again."

"You think it is a serial killer?" Kent asked. "Appears to be," George agreed.

"Well, maybe this time the guy made a mistake," Kent said as he walked over to view the body. He looked at the body. "Pretty girl, wasn't she? What a pity."

"I can't help but notice that she resembles the first girl," George replied. "About the same height, nice figure, brunette and similar hairstyle."

"You may have something there," Kent agreed. He walked over to one of the forensic guys. "Can you tell me the time of death?"

"Well, based on the cold temperature, I would say sometime last night maybe after 10 o'clock. We will know more after we get to the morgue."

George walked up to Kent. "Saturday is typically a date night; she may have been on a date."

"Yeah, first we need to know who she was dating." Kent said "Maybe it was a date that went wrong. But since this place appears to be the guy's dumping ground, it probably is the same guy."

"First we need to ID her. I didn't see any clothes or purse," George replied.

"Any tattoos or identifying marks?"

"None that I could see – but I only saw her backside." George confessed. He looked at the forensic guys as they placed the body in a body bag and put her on a gurney. He turned to the forensic guy, "What did you see on her front?"

"Someone beat her up pretty good, especially on her face. Then it looks like she was raped and then strangled." The forensic guy looked at George. "You guys have to catch this guy."

"Yes," George responded as he watched the forensic team walk away.

"Why do you think he beats them?" Kent asked.

"I don't know, could be that he enjoys doing it or maybe he thinks it will be harder to identify them." George walked over to where the body had been placed but he could not see anything in the way of a clue.

"Well. It had to happen before the snow storm or we would see his tracks."

"It started snowing around 11pm last night so his estimate of the time of death might be pretty accurate." George noted.

"Let's hope he made a mistake this time. We have to catch this monster," Kent remarked as he walked back to his car.

George stood there for a while and then walked to his patrol car. We've got to catch and stop this son of a bitch, he thought to himself.

CHAPTER 32

Ron was at his desk putting the finishing touches on his qualification test report. Harvey Johnson came out of his office and noted that everyone was there.

"I have an announcement," he started "We are starting the endurance test in the static test frame this week. Everyone will be monitoring this test in 12-hour shifts. You will be paid overtime for the extra hours you work. I am handing out a signup sheet so you can choose which days you can work. This is a three week test so I need every one here to select which days you are available for each week. We will also have some volunteers from the engineering department down the hill to help out." The early shift was from 6 am to 6 pm. The late shift was from 6 pm to 6 am.

He gave the sheet to Stan Welland. It was passed around the office until it finally came to Ron. The only days left were late shifts on Friday, Saturday, Sunday and Monday and Tuesday. Ron selected the late shifts for Monday and Tuesday, not wanting to mess up his weekends with Sue at the campus. The list was then sent up the hill to receive the volunteer engineers sign ups. Ron was glad that the lab guys got first picks.

When Penny received the signup list, she noted that Ron had avoided the weekend slots. She made some quick changes to the list and then passed the sign-up sheets to the fourth floor design group to see if anyone wanted extra overtime. Luckily there were enough design guys who wanted the extra overtime. The final list results were posted on Harvey's office door. When Ron checked the list he saw that he was scheduled for the early shift on Saturday and the late shift on Sunday. He couldn't believe his eyes. These shifts basically ruined his weekends for the next three weeks. He went and protested to Harvey.

"These aren't the shifts I signed up for." He showed Harvey the list.

"Well, I'm sorry, but you have the least seniority so you have to take the shifts assigned to you," Harvey explained.

"It's not fair," Ron protested.

"Life is not always fair. Suck it up this time." Harvey dismissed him. He was sorry the kid got a bad assignment but there was nothing he could do about it.

Ron was upset. These old buildings had steel roofs so no one had cell phone signals inside. He walked outside and called Sue. He wanted to tell her the bad news.

"Hello," She saw Ron's name on her caller ID. "I am so glad you called, we are having a chemistry test next week and I need you to show me how to balance these equations…" she started.

"Listen…I have bad news. I am going to be tied up on this endurance test for three weeks." He tried to remain calm while talking to her. "I won't be able to come home on the weekends."

"Oh no…" she exclaimed.

"I am sorry but there's nothing I can do about it." The frustration showed in his voice.

"Three whole weeks?" She could feel his frustration.

"I will make it up to you, I promise. I am going to talk to my old engineering boss and ask for a transfer back to the design group."

"Ok…I understand," she replied sadly. She hung up. This long distance relationship was starting to worry her. She believed that he was being truthful but it did cause doubts. She would have to study the chemistry assignment harder. Most of the stuff about different electron levels of the elements in the periodic table just did not make sense to her. Her non-analytic artistic mind was having a hard time with the complicated concepts of chemistry. Why did have to be so hard?

CHAPTER 33

Detective Kent and George Coleman were at the city morgue. They were awaiting the report on the dead girl by the city medical examiner. Dr. John Fraiser came out of his office to meet them.

"Well, the girl was beaten severely, raped and then strangled, possibly in that order," he read from his clipboard. "The same M.O. as the girl killed on campus last month. There was evidence that she had been tasered at least twice. There was tape residue on her arms just like the first girl. Apparently her arms were taped together behind her sometime in the process."

"Any chance to identify her?" Detective Kent asked. "How about checking her with facial recognition compared to the college ID card database?" All students had picture ID to carry with them on campus.

"We tried that last time, but there was so much facial damage that we couldn't find a match," Dr. Fraiser explained. "We did get a DNA sample of the rapist – I am pretty sure it will be the same as the first case."

"So, we don't know anything yet," Kent replied.

"Well, I can tell you that the two victims were very similar, both were about five feet eight with brown hair and green eyes. They were both Caucasian and had trim figures, probably very sexy. It appears that the killer has a taste for this type of female," the doctor related.

"That could limit the number of possible victims on campus if he is a serial killer," George replied. "There can't be that many women on campus that fit that description."

"That may be true if she is an actual student. She may be from the city and not a student," Detective Kent noted.

"Well, I am going back to campus. If she was a student, she may have a roommate that may come forward to report a missing person." George turned to walk away.

"Keep me informed," Kent called after him.

"Ditto," George replied. As he walked to his police car he thought to himself that this was turning out to be a real nightmare. The campus was supposed to be a peaceful environment for learning, not a killing field. He was grateful for the city police who were assisting him but felt that he was not doing his duty to protect the students on campus. It was true that the city police were as puzzled as he was, but that did not make him feel any better. He knew he was not a trained detective, but felt that this mess was somehow his fault. He knew that this second killing would be in the newspaper and people were going to be clamoring for the police to catch the killer. They may even want him to be fired and replaced with someone more competent. He decided to visit the Dean of the college and ask to hire a couple of more officers.

CHAPTER 34

Ron Pritchard was monitoring the static frame test at work. It was a boring job since the cycling of the test part was operateded by an automatic controller. Someone had to be present in case the part broke or for some reason the loads exceeded the requirement or a hydraulic line ruptured. So, he sat at a desk behind the 1-inch thick window of bullet proof plexiglas where he could watch the instrumentation readouts. The chair next to him was empty. It was about 8 PM on a Saturday night. Everything appeared to be running well and he was alone in the lab. If something did go wrong he had a kill switch to hit near his hand on the desk. The hardest part was staying awake. He also had to take periodic readings and record them in a notebook. A video camera was also watching the test and recording the cycles as the part was being tested by two large 8-inch diameter actuators that were being pressurized at 2000 psig. He was plainly bored but still kept watch, not wanting to miss any test anomalies. He was still upset about having to work the weekends but understood that he was low man on the seniority list.

"Hello." He was surprised to hear a voice behind him and he sort of jumped. He turned around and saw Penny standing there, dressed in tan slacks and a brown jacket. She had her hair up and clipped in place instead of her typical long free flowing hairstyle. She was still stunningly beautiful even in casual dress. She had a paper bag in her hand.

"Hi," he said. "What are you doing here?" he asked in a friendly tone. He was totally surprised to see her.

"I wanted to stop by and apologize for putting you on weekend duty." She smiled at him. "The bosses decided who would get the times based on seniority," she lied.

"That's ok. I understand." He smiled back at her.

"I thought I could make it up to you by bringing you a snack." She sat in the empty chair and opened the bag. Inside were two plastic containers with a cheesecake dessert and two cups of coffee. She offered a container and cup to him. "I didn't know how you liked your coffee." She said as she handed him a plastic fork.

"Well, thanks…but I don't drink coffee, but tea." He pushed the cup away. "I do like cheesecake though, thanks."

"Oh…sorry," she replied.

"That's ok," he said seeing she was disappointed. "It was awful nice of you to bring me a snack." He opened the container. It had a cherry cheesecake in it, one of his favorites.

"That's ok," Penny smiled at him as he dug into the cheesecake. "I wanted to see you again and thought this would be a good time." She put her hand on his arm.

"Oh. Well, thanks." He was really surprised that such a pretty girl would be interested in him. He was engaged though, and figured he needed to tell her. "I am sort of engaged to a girl back home," he said in a low voice.

"That's ok, we can still be friends," she said, not surprised at his statement.

"Sure." He noted that she was still smiling at him. Wow. He thought she would get up and leave when she heard he was engaged but she was still sitting there, smiling at him. They ate the cheesecake in silence.

"Do you like working here?" she asked, and drank some coffee.

"Yeah, I always wanted to work at an aerospace company. I was an intern here two summers ago and really liked it," he replied.

"Well, I heard you were doing a good job here." She finished the coffee.

"Yeah, but I really want to get back in the design group."

"Well, that may happen sooner than you think." She looked at him with her eyes fixed on his. She smiled again. "Well, I've got to be going." She stood up and put her arm around him and kissed him on the cheek. She turned to walk away. "I will see you later." She purred.

"Ok." He was shocked by the kiss. He turned to see her walk away in a sexy manner. What just happened? he thought. I told her I was engaged and it did not seem to matter to her. He turned back to the test but had a hard time concentrating on the job. He immediately thought that he should call Sue, but the steel roofs in these old buildings cut off the signal to his cell phone. Maybe later, he thought.

CHAPTER 35

George Coleman was sitting in his office at the police station. It was Tuesday afternoon and he still had no identification for the second victim that had been killed Saturday night. He hoped she was not a student on campus, but no one had reported anyone missing yet. He noticed a female student entering the office and talking to Andy Hall at the dispatch desk. She was wearing slacks and a topcoat. Andy quickly motioned for George to join them. George got up and walked over to them.

"She says her roommate has not returned to their dorm room," Andy explained

"Yes, I went home for the weekend and my roommate had a date on Friday but was not there when I returned today," the girl told George.

"What is your name?" George asked.

"I am Mary Brown and I live in Spenser Hall. I know she had classes today but she has not even returned from the date. Her books are still on her desk."

"What is your roommate's name?" George asked. Apparently she did not know about the murder yet.

"Her name is Barbara Perry."

"Do you have a recent photo of her?" he asked. She took out her phone and found a picture and showed it to him. She really looked a lot like victim number two. Geoge looked at the girl. "I am afraid I have some bad news for you. We found a girl in the woods by the Student Union and she looks a lot like your roommate."

"Barb?" she started crying. "Please tell me it's not Barb."

"Can you identify her for us?" he asked.

"I suppose so…" she tried to stop crying.

"Who was she dating?" he asked.

"It was someone we met in the Student Union from Harvey High school; I think she said his name was Frank Starkey."

Andy and George drove Mary to the city Morgue. They entered the building and ran into Detective Kent who was waiting to see them. Dr. Fraser was also waiting for them.

"Do we have a possible name?" Detective Kent asked.

"Let her see the girl first," Dr. Fraser replied, "This way," he led them into the examination room. A body was on the table, covered with an opaque white sheet. They all gathered around as Dr. Fraser lifted the sheet to show the victim's face. Although she had been beaten, Dr. Fraser had cleaned up her face somewhat. When Mary saw the face, she started crying and turned away.

"Yes…it is…Barb," she said between sobs.

"So, her name is Barbara Perry," George informed Detective Kent. "Maybe this will help us catch this guy. We have the name of the guy she dated on Saturday." George and Andy walked out of the building with Mary and Kent.

"Well, that's a start," Kent agreed.

"His name is Frank Starkey and he supposedly attended Harvey High school." George informed him. I should know more as I interview the roommate more."

"Ok. I will check with Harvey High school," Detective Kent replied. "Is that in Ohio?"

"I think it is in Lake County, in Painesville," Andy replied. "I used to go to high school in Mentor and Painesville is right next door." Mary was somewhat subdued but agreed with Andy.

"We should be able to get this guy now." George and Andy escorted Mary back to their squad car. George hated that the young girl had been killed but maybe they now had a solid lead to check out.

CHAPTER 36

Sue Conner was walking to her chemistry class. She had heard of the second murder and was being very cautious about walking on campus. She really missed Ron and had hoped he would have returned over the weekend to help her with this course. She heard footsteps behind her and turned suddenly in a karate defense stance.

"Hi Sue." It was Greg Sommers.

"Hi Greg," she responded. She lowered her guard.

"Did you hear about the second murder?" he asked.

"Yes...it's terrible."

"Then why are you walking around campus unescorted?" he asked.

"Well, I do have a third degree black belt in karate...I think I can defend myself."

"Ok, but you don't mind if I walk with you?" he asked.

"No, that's ok. I am going to the Parker building for a class," she replied.

"That's next to Crawford Hall, I am headed that way anyway," he agreed.

"So how are you doing here at school?'

"I am doing ok. The business classes are not that hard. Math class is the hardest course for me. How about you?" he asked.

"I am really struggling with chemistry." she admitted. "Ron was supposed to help me but he is tied up at work in Cleveland."

"That's too bad. Sorry that I can't help you with that. I did terrible in high school chemistry, barely got a 'D,'" he explained.

"Well, it was nice to see you again," she said as she stopped in front of the Parker building.

"Yeah, see you around," he walked off.

She remembered him from high school; they had dated a few times, but never really hit it off. He was way too aggressive and tried to get her to go to bed with him. She broke it off and they did not see each other much after that. She did not remember knowing that he took chemistry. She did not take any of those technical classes, staying with the Fine Arts curriculum. With some determination she entered the building and went to class.

CHAPTER 37

*H*e *had enjoyed the second girl very much. But it was still somewhat disappointing that she was nothing like the girl he had an obsession for. The girls he selected were close to her physically but just did not have the personality he had obsessed over. Still, they were entertaining for the short term. When they did not submit to him he shocked them with his 'stinger' which paralyzed them. They were still conscious and aware of him but could not move for several minutes. He would take this opportunity to undress them and tape their arms behind their back. Then he had his way with them and when they tried to struggle he would beat them until they submitted. They typically started to cry and bawl a lot as he used and abused them. To quiet them he simply strangled them. But that was not what he wanted. He wanted to possess them for a period of time so he could keep abusing them. But when they cried, he lost control of his temper and killed them. Then there was the problem of disposing of the body. The street behind the student union was a perfect place to park his car and carry the body into the forest. There were no houses on that street so no one saw his car. When he had walked almost to the other side, he deposited the body. He kept their purses since it was sort of a trophy. Now he only had two more targets to approach. If his plan worked he should be able to satisfy his obsession. He licked his lips in anticipation.*

CHAPTER 38

George Coleman looked at the city paper. The headline blared 'NO PROGRESS IN FINDING CAMPUS MURDERER.' Every lead they had was a dead end. There was no record of a Frank Starkey attending the college or ever attending Harvey High School. It was apparently an alias made up by the killer. Although the murdered girl's roommate had seen him talking to her friend Barbara, she could not accurately describe him. He looked average, average height and build. She only saw him from behind so she could not sit with a police artist to make a sketch. The only things that were similar between the women is that they were physically similar in build, hair style and having green eyes. They both had stayed in a dormitory at Spenser Hall. That one fact had instigated a careful search of the building to see if any evidence existed about the killer. That had been a dismal failure. The killer's DNA was another dead end. Apparently he had never been put in the system and did not have any close relatives in the DNA databases. They had investigated the last victims' internet entries and had seen that she had mentioned 'Frank' as being a nice guy she had met in the Student Union but did not provide any data about him that would be useable to the investigation. A police profiler had determined that the killer was probably a male Caucasian in his late 20s with a persuasive personality with a sadistic tendency to be cruel and possibly a psychopath. This was not news to George who already figured out the type of monster the guy was. How any guy could take a pretty girl and do the things the killer did to her was beyond his comprehension. In his mind, women were wonderful, marvelous, intelligent creatures that he could not possibly harm but had to protect. Probably one of the reasons he had opted for a career in crime prevention. In this case though, he was helpless to prevent these attacks. It bothered him so much; he was losing sleep over it. He had increased the patrolling on campus and had hired two additional patrolmen since the dean of the college had increased his budget in an attempt to stop the killings. He knew it was not enough and he dreaded the next killing. He called Kent to touch base.

CHAPTER 39

It was a Tuesday evening. Sue was in her dormitory room trying to study the Chemistry problems. She had asked Joan, her roommate if she had ever taken Chemistry.

"No, I avoided that course." Joan replied. "I thought Ron was going to help you with that stuff?"

"He would if he was here, but he is tied up on a test in his new job."

"I wondered why you haven't been going out the last couple of weeks," Joan replied. "Well, he should be coming home this weekend," Sue noted as she tried to balance an equation. "How are you and Jerry doing?"

"He is taking a more serious attempt at getting good grades this semester. We still go out but not as often. We are being cautious with a killer on the loose on campus." Joan sat on her bunk.

"The killer is targeting girls, why would Jerry be afraid?"

"He is not really afraid; he just wants us to keep a low profile. When we are out, he never leaves my side," Joan explained.

"Sounds like he wants to protect you." Sue closed her book. She would try working the chemistry problems again tomorrow when she went to the library. As it was getting late, she changed into her pajamas and sat on her bed.

"I think that Jerry is not quite sure what to do if we are confronted. He isn't a fighter and doesn't carry a weapon like Ron does." Joan pulled back the covers and slipped into bed. "And he does not have a third degree black belt like you do."

"Still, I don't think you have anything to worry about if you stick together." Sue got up to turn out the lights. She walked over to the door to make sure it was locked.

"You're probably right," Joan said sleepily.

"I think that everyone is getting paranoid," Sue replied slipping into bed. The small nightlight near the door to the bathroom was just bright enough to allow them to walk around the room without bumping into anything in the dark. Sue lay in bed but was still awake. She had never had problems with school work before. But now she was totally lost trying to figure out Chemistry. She really missed not having Ron around, not so much for the help with Chemistry but because she was deeply in love with him. They had been lovers for about 6 months now and she really missed him not being here. He was so kind and gentle and never got upset with her. If they had a problem, he immediately tried to resolve the issue without getting upset. He would always find a compromise that was acceptable to both of them. She had never met a man with such a calm temperament. His involvement with the campus police force as an auxiliary policeman had helped stop a campus rapist last summer. That was the only time that she knew that he had lost his control and attacked the criminal to bring him down. Now that man was in prison for several years. She wished that Ron was still in school sometimes, so that they could be together. She felt the ring on her finger. It had been Ron's mothers' ring and he had given it to her when he asked her to marry him. It was comforting to her that he had pledged to love her forever, but he wasn't here. She wondered about what her father had told them about a long distance relationship. She hoped that they would be able to maintain their relationship in spite of what her father had said. Although she felt bad about Ron's absence, she eventually turned over and went to sleep.

CHAPTER 40

Ron was walking down the hill from the test lab to the main office building. It was a windy but sunny day for March. The temperature was about 50 but the wind made it feel like 40. He was not sure why he was being called to the engineering office. He hoped it was not bad news. Although he did not like working in the test lab, he was trying to make the best of it. In his short time there he had learned a lot about the products the company made. In his spare time, he had walked through the manufacturing plant and saw several products in their unfinished condition and thought it was fascinating. As he got to the employee gate, he slid his picture badge across the sensor and a green light came on, meaning he could push the gate open to enter. As he stepped inside he walked down the hallway to the main elevator. The security guard was at his desk and looked over to see Ron. He nodded and said hello. Ron said hello also as he pushed the button for the fourth floor. He got off at the fourth floor and was near the Engineering Vice President's office. He looked at his watch, he was about five minutes early but walked in anyway. Penny was sitting at her desk looking at her computer screen. She noticed him and looked up.

"Hello Ron." She smiled at him. "He is ready for you; you can go right in."

"Thanks." He opened the door. Jeff Tyler was sitting at a chair facing Lou Roberts who was sitting on the other side of the desk.

"Come in and sit down." Lou pointed at the remaining chair. "I hear you have been doing good work in the test lab," Lou started. "I have been talking to Jeff and reviewing your college transcripts. It appears that you got straight A's in computer programing and calculus. He motioned to papers on his desk.

"Yes sir." Ron sat down. "They were easy courses." Ron wasn't telling the whole truth. He had dropped calculus twice and only on his third try did he figure it out.

"Well, I have a special project that requires someone well versed in computer simulations who can develop a calculus solution to accurize a simulation that will let us design this device:" He spread a drawing out on his desk. The device contained a piston in a cylinder attached to a shaft. "We need to be able to change the dimensions to provide an accurate load, but the upper chamber is pressurized with air. As the piston moves, the pressure changes as the volume is compressed. You think this would be simple, but the bottom half has an orifice that meters the high pressure input flow and pushes the piston. As the piston moves, the reaction at the orifice changes due to the reaction of the air pressure," Lou explained. No one in engineering has been able to figure this out. The load and stroke have to be as specified. We have tested several iterations but even Stan Welland hasn't been able to get close."

"I told Lou that someone fresh out of college who had recently taken these courses might be able to solve the problem," Jeff Tyler explained.

"Yes. I want you to move back to Engineering and try to come up with a calculus equation we can use for this simulation," Lou looked at Ron expectantly.

Well...I could try I suppose." Ron looked at the drawing.

"Good. Start right away. Jeff, give this man a desk and access to the computer terminal." Lou rolled up the drawing and gave it to Ron.

"Ok. Ron, let's go." Jeff stood up and headed for the door.

Ron followed reluctantly. He wondered if he actually could correct the simulation. As they left Lou's office Penney saw them head into the design area. She was hoping that Ron would now be working in the design group where she would have easier access to him. Now she could finally put her plan in place.

Jeff set Ron up with a desk and a computer terminal. He had an IT person set up Ron's sign in and password for the computer. Then he showed Ron the initial computer program that had inputs for the simulation.

"We got it to run but it always blows up after the high pressure flow starts," Jeff explained. "Good luck," he said as he walked away.

"Thanks," Ron replied. Ron spread out the drawings and looked at the basic design. He wondered what he had gotten himself into. This problem was probably unsolvable. Everything had to be sized to provide the required reaction load on the part. If the load was too high the part would fail. If it did not provide the correct load, the device would not work and the aircraft probably would not operate as specified. And finding a calculus equation that would provide a proper simulation would be very difficult since there were too many variables to consider. He held his head in his hands as he leaned on the desk. He did not even know where to start.

CHAPTER 41

*H*e was stalking the nursing student. He had been watching her for several weeks and had become familiar with her schedule. She was basically almost always with a crowd of students which made her inaccessible. There was one day a week where she was alone for about a half hour as she visited a store in the city. She always walked back the same way and entered the campus at the same place on a path near a wooded area. He figured that if he surprised her there he could then drag her into the woods and have his way with her. The timing was the problem. She never left or returned at the same time. Typically, it was a Wednesday since she did not have any classes that day. She always went to the same store and bought weekly supplies of snacks and fruit that she obviously snacked on during the week in her dorm room. He also was watching the Art student but she could wait. He really wanted to get the nursing student. She was really sexy looking and had drawn the attention of several male students but she did not go out with any of them. He began to wonder if perhaps she was gay. Or possibly she didn't want any distractions in her coursework. Perhaps she was afraid that one the men that approached her was the murderer. She seemed to have several girl friends around her when she went to class. They were probably sticking together because of him and the two previous girls he had killed. It seemed that everyone one on campus was tense and nervous. He finally figured out a plan to get the girl. Tomorrow was Wednesday and she was bound to go to the store again. He could hardly wait. He would meet her on the path through the forest.

CHAPTER 42

It was early evening. Sue and Joan were at the library studying after having a light supper in their dorm room. Sue was trying to figure out the chemistry problems and Joan was doing research for a paper for one of her classes. The semester was almost over and they were neither doing as well as they had hoped. Sue was at the point where she either had to hire a tutor or hope that Ron came home this weekend to help her. Joan could have picked an easier topic for her term paper. She was having trouble finding much information on the topic she had selected. Sue was thinking that she was finally getting the knack of balancing the practice equation she was working on but when she checked the answer in the back of the book she had done it wrong. So, she tried to back calculate the problem from knowing what the answer was but that did not seem to work either. She was getting really frustrated. Joan was not having much luck either.

"Hi Sue, Hi Joan." Greg Sommers walked by their table and stopped to chat.

"Hi Greg. What brings you to the library?" Joan asked.

"I was looking up a business case to use in my marketing class," he explained.

"Did you find it?" Sue asked, still frustrated with the chemistry problem.

"Yeah…It is a good one." He turned to leave but stopped. "You guys want to give it a break and go to the Dairy Queen?" he asked.

"Well, that sounds good, but I've got to get this report done," Joan replied.

"Yeah… I just have to complete my work, so no." Sue turned him down.

"Ok, maybe next time." He turned and walked away.

"That was nice of him to offer," Joan said.

"Yeah, I think he may have changed since high school. He was sort of pushy back then." Sue turned to Joan. "Do you think he was hitting on us?"

"No… He seems to be pretty harmless," Joan replied.

"He has been friendlier than I remember from high school."

"Yes, he seems to have matured somewhat," Joan agreed.

They continued to study for about another hour and as it started to get dark they decided to pack it in for the night and walk back to the dorm. It was dark enough that the lights along the path came on. It was getting much colder now that the sun had gone down. It was about 40 degrees and getting colder. As they walked, they talked about the upcoming weekend. Joan wanted to know if she and Jerry could double date with Sue and Ron if he came home. Sue was reluctant to make plans that would involve Ron. They had not seen each other for three weeks and he just might want to do something romantic. At least she was hoping that would be the case. She told Joan that she would see what plans Ron had and get back to her on that. As they rounded a corner they saw a dark figure run into the bushes about 30 yards ahead of them. They immediately stopped.

"Did you see that?" Joan asked.

"Yes…you don't think…?"

"It just might be…" Joan didn't want to say the murderer. She was too scared to say much of anything.

"It probably is just someone out running for exercise." Sue tried to remain calm and hoped Joan would not panic.

"At night?" Joan asked starting to get hysterical.

"I don't want to leave the path. Let's keep going. He won't attack if there are two of us," Sue replied.

"I'm not so sure." Joan reached down and brought a steak knife out of her sock. They both wore slacks in the wintertime and she had mid-calf socks on underneath.

"Where did you get that?" Sue asked, shocked at seeing the knife.

"I started to carry it in my sock right after the first murder." Joan pointed the knife at the bushes.

"OK." Sue was impressed. She had always relied on her karate training to protect herself and had not thought about a weapon. They continued to walk down the path but nothing happened. "Maybe he is afraid of the knife," Sue whispered.

"I hope so," Joan replied.

They made it back to their dorm without any events. Joan had returned the knife to her sock before they entered the dorm. Sue was not unhappy that Joan had been prepared. She was not sure that Joan could actually bring herself to stab someone, but you never knew what someone would do when facing a dangerous encounter.

"Well, we made it back ok." Sue opened the door to their dorm room.

"Yeah, it was probably nothing," Joan sighed. "Do you think we should report it to the campus police?"

"I'm not sure of what exactly we saw...it was very dark." Sue took off her coat and hung it in the closet. "What could we tell them? Can you describe the guy?"

"No...it was too dark. I guess we shouldn't report it." Joan also hung up her coat.

CHAPTER 43

George Coleman was sitting at his desk in the campus police station, reading reports from the city detectives in their efforts to find the killer. So far they had no viable leads. Everything turned out to be a dead end. The city police cars were even now patrolling the areas around the campus. Increased presence of more police on campus was becoming more common. The students noticed this as a reminder that a killer was loose on campus. A dramatic reduction in parties was evidence that the young women students were staying in their dorms during the weekends. Even the fraternities stopped having parties which was a surprise to George. It had been almost a month since the last attack and George was under a lot of stress since he was expecting a third attack but hoped it would not occur. He was hoping that the increased police presence would scare the bad guy away. Several 24-hour video cameras had been installed on the buildings, monitoring the various pathways around campus. The students had noticed the additional surveillance but had accepted it. He only had one guy to monitor the various camera feeds and he only worked an eight hour shift. Still, if an attack did occur, they would be able to review the footage which was recorded and saved for seven days. It was getting late, almost 6:00 PM. He noticed that Andy Hall had returned from his patrol. There was a woman student with him. He motioned for George to join them.

"Hi Andy. You are back early from your patrol," George greeted them.

"George, you better listen to her story," Andy was frowning,

"Hello." He turned to the young woman. He was hoping it was not what he thought it was. "What's your name?" he asked.

The girl was dressed in a black jacket and blue jeans. She had blond hair and a stocking cap on. It was still pretty cold for the end of March.

"I am Margie Turner and my roommate has not returned to our room. I am worried that she may have…." She didn't finish but started to cry.

"Ok, what is her name?" George asked calmly. He was dreading that another girl had become a victim of the "Campus Strangler" (as the local paper called the killer).

"Her name is Patty, Patty Sinclair, my roommate…she is a student in the nursing program…We are both in the nursing program…" she said between sobs.

"Lets' not jump to conclusions," George said quietly. "When did you last see her?" he inquired.

"She was in the dorm this morning, left to go do some shopping around noon but never came back. She always comes back in about an hour." The young woman had calmed down a little.

"Is it possible that she had a date with someone?" George asked. He knew this was the typical M.O. of the strangler.

"No…she broke up with her boyfriend last summer and she hasn't dated anyone since."

"Maybe she ran into some friends and visited their dorm." Andy tried to help steer away from the killer scenario.

"She would have called me if that was the case. We are best friends," Margie replied, drying her eyes with a tissue that Andy offered.

"Well, she has only been gone a few hours, maybe she decided to do more shopping." George replied. "Have you tried to call her?"

"When she didn't return as normal, I tried calling her but there was no answer."

"Maybe her cell phone was off?" Andy asked.

"No, she is careful to have it on when she travels around campus. She is afraid of the killer so she is extra careful."

"Ok, we will put out an alert. But she has been missing for only a few hours so she probably will show up at your dorm." George tried to reassure her. "Which dorm are you in?"

"We are in the Bennings building, second floor, Room 210." She had stopped crying.

"Ok, we will check back with you but there might be a simple explanation. She may have returned while you came over here. Andy, please drive her back to her dorm."

"Will do." Andy escorted her out to his patrol car. George was sure it was just a non-event. At least he hoped so. He grabbed his coat and hat and walked out to his police car. On the way he called Detective Kent.

"We may have another missing girl," he explained to Kent.

"Are you sure?" Kent inquired.

"No, but I am going over to the woods by the Student Union to check it out." Since both victims were found in basically the same spot, they had installed a video camera there, just in case the killer was determined to use that site.

"Let me know if you find her," Detective Kent replied.

"Will do." George drove over to the woods near the student union. He got out of the patrol car and walked over to the woods. He hesitated to enter the woods just to find another victim. Andy Hall drove up and parked behind George's car. George waited for Andy to join him.

"The missing girl has not returned to her dorm," Andy reported.

"Ok...let's start looking," George replied. They entered and walked over to the site where the first two women were found. Although they were prepared for the worst, there was no body.

"Do you think he saw the camera?" Andy pointed up to an adjacent tree.

"I doubt it. You hardly ever look up if you are walking in the woods." George looked up to the camera. "Maybe he put her somewhere else this time. We should search the whole area." They continued the search of the woods but after a couple of hours they were sure there was no body in the wooded area. George's cell phone rang. It was detective Kent.

"Did you find her?" Kent asked.

"No…no body in these woods. It could be a false alarm or maybe he hasn't finished with her yet. We will station a man here to watch. I will check the video record to see if he checked out the site and maybe saw the camera," George replied.

"Well maybe he hasn't struck again. I bet the missing girl shows up."

"God, I hope you are right." George hung up. "Andy, please stick around for a couple of hours. I will send Patrick to relieve you at ten." It was already getting dark and was getting colder.

"Ok but I want to get my night vision goggles from my car." Andy started to walk back to the car. George stood at the edge of the woods and wondered if the girl was really missing or not. He hoped she was just visiting a friend or something. Since it was cold, Andy had a fur-lined coat on. He would be ok if he stayed alert and awake. George told him to report in every 30 minutes on his cell phone. George drove back to the police station. When he got there, he saw that everyone had left except officer Patrick who was on night duty. He told Patrick to go over to the Student Union woods at ten o'clock to relieve Andy.

"How late should I stay?" Patrick asked.

"Only until midnight. Take your pistol with you. I will cover the desk here until then." George was not used to doing a double shift but felt he had to today. He called Miss Turner to ask if her roommate had returned.

"No, she hasn't returned … I'm getting very worried," she sounded as if she was panicked.

"Well, call me on my cell phone when she returns." George tried to sound calm.

"OK." She hung up.

George was supposed to have dinner with Jennifer tonight and had forgotten in the search for the missing girl. He called Jennifer.

"Jen, I'm sorry about dinner…we have another missing girl," he said when she answered the phone.

"Oh no…I understand. Please tell me she hasn't been killed," Jen answered softly.

"We haven't found her. It may be a false alarm but we cannot rule out anything at this time," George replied. His voice was low, and she could tell that he was tired.

"You want to stop over?" she asked.

"I have to be here until midnight. We are stationing a man at the site where we found the first two bodies. I'll try to see you tomorrow sometime."

"Ok. Please be careful?" she implored.

"Always." He hung up. He knew that Jen understood that the police job sometime took extra hours. He was very tired but kept awake until Patrick returned.

"Nobody showed up." Patrick reported.

"Let's hope the girl shows up and is ok," George replied as he started to get ready to leave.

CHAPTER 44

*H*e smiled with satisfaction. It had worked just as he had planned it. It was an overcast day with thick winter clouds in the sky. It was a brisk 50 degrees but hardly any wind. He saw her coming down the path towards him. They were both entering the wooded area and would meet about in the middle. He did not see any one else on the path. She was wearing blue jeans and a light tan jacket. She had a stocking cap on but the back of her neck was exposed. She had a plastic bag of groceries in her left hand and a cell phone in her right. Her purse was on a strap over her shoulder. He had a backpack on like most of the students. As he approached her he pretended to be using his cell phone and texting away madly. She at first stopped when she saw him but he acted as if he did not even see her. As he came close he almost bumped into her but moved past, obviously intent on the message on the cell phone. He said "Excuse me," politely. She turned to watch him pass but then turned back onto the path. He quickly turned and hit her with the stinger right on her exposed neck. She crumpled down on the path, paralyzed. He quickly looked both ways along the path but no one was coming in either direction. He grabbed her arms and dragged her into the woods about a hundred feet. There was a hollow in the terrain that was out of sight from the path. The trees were thick enough anyway but he had picked out this site ahead of time. She had a look of terror on her face. He went back and retrieved her bag of groceries and her cell phone. She had started to text 911 but had not had time to send it. He made sure no one was coming on the path again and returned to the girl. She was starting to recover so he zapped her again. He took a blanket from his backpack and spread it on the ground. Then he took a roll of gray tape from the backpack and positioned the girl on the blanket so that her arms would reach to two adjacent sapling trees. He taped her hands to each of the trees. He spread her legs and used the tape to tie each foot to two other trees. He took a bandana and raised her head to put the gag over her mouth so she wouldn't cry out. She was trying to say something so he waited.

"Please…please do whatever you want…just don't kill me. I will let you do what you want," she pleaded desperately.

He put the bandana over her mouth and tied it behind her head. "Ok honey, if you don't struggle I will let you live," he lied. It was nice that she was cooperating but it was sort of a disappointment to him also. He liked to have total control over his victims. He started to undress her. Since she was restrained he used a razor knife to cut through her blouse and jeans. Then he cut off her undergarments in the same manner. Now she was naked except for her socks and shoes which were covered with tape. Her eyes were wide and full of fear. He then raped her violently as she tried to scream but her voice was muted by the gag in her mouth. After he was finished, he looked at her. "I know I said I would let you live but I can't have you identifying me can I?" She muffled some words as loud as she could but he couldn't understand what she was saying. He put his hands around her neck and strangled her. He looked around and picked up his stuff. He didn't want to leave any trace of himself. He managed to remove the blanket and rolled it up and replaced it in the backpack with the roll of tape. The stinger went into his coat pocket. He had used it twice. It would need to be recharged before the next time. He looked at her cell phone, stepped on it and smashed it. Then he threw it as far away as he could. He left the bag of groceries but put her purse in his backpack. Satisfied that he had cleaned the site, he removed the gag from her mouth. It was bloody where she had cut her mouth trying to scream. He put it in a plastic bag and would dispose of it later. He walked out of the woods on a different route than they had entered. As he came out of the woods he looked both *ways but there was nobody on the path. He walked back toward campus but turned to go into the first parking lot. His car was where he left it. He drove into the city and parked in an alley where he dumped the blanket and gag in an open dumpster, covering it with some other trash. Again no one was around to see him. He drove to his city apartment. He was satiated for the moment. He always had a feeling of elation afterward. Three down, one to go he thought.*

CHAPTER 45

Sue Conner was pacing back and forth in her dorm room. She was wearing a low-cut T- shirt and blue jeans. It was almost eight o'clock on Friday night. Ron had called her earlier and said he was finally returning to campus after being absent for three weeks.

"Why are you so nervous?" Joan asked from across room.

"He said he would be here. He should have gotten here by now. If he said he would come, he will. You know he wouldn't lie to you," Joan noted. "He is probably more eager to see you than you are to see him."

"Maybe. But if he left work at four, he should have been here by now." There was a knock on the door. Sue ran to the door and flung it open. Ron rushed in and took her in his arms and they kissed. It was a long kiss with a lot of fondling.

"Ahem…" Joan tried to get their attention. They slowly parted and turned to see Joan.

"Sorry about that," Ron started.

"I'm not," Sue said, still holding tightly on to Ron.

"Well, maybe I should go downstairs?" Joan asked.

"No need. We were just going to get something to eat. Want to come along?" Ron asked.

"I better not. I might get in the way." Joan turned back toward her bed, smiling.

"That's ok," Sue said as she grabbed her coat. They headed out the door and were gone.

"Where are we going?" Sue asked as they ran down the stairs and out to his Jeep. "Most places are closing by now."

"Remember our favorite diner down the street from my place? They are open until 10 pm. I'm hungry and need to eat something," Ron replied, opening the car door for her.

"Sounds good to me," Sue agreed.

"I thought you would be here a lot sooner," Sue started to complain.

"Sorry, I was working on a difficult problem and lost track of time," he explained.

"Well, you are here...we have the rest of the weekend."

"Yes...I probably need to get away from the problem. Sometimes if I do that my subconscious comes up with a solution when I sleep," Ron explained.

"Really? Is that how engineers figure out problems?" she asked.

"Not for everybody but it sometimes works for me," he replied.

"Well, I am continuously learning more and more about you."

"I hope you are happy with what you learn," he smiled.

"I am quite happy with the person I am in love with."

They stopped at the diner and had a quick meal. Afterward they ended up in his apartment for some intimate coupling. Ron was so exhausted that he passed out and could not take Sue back to the dorm. She did not complain but lay there watching him sleep until she fell asleep also. In the morning they would have to explain to his landlord why he had an overnight guest.

CHAPTER 46

George Coleman was sitting in his office at the campus police department. It had been three days since Patty Sinclair had gone missing. Her roommate was calling him daily with requests for progress. He and the city police had issued an all-points bulletin for the girl and her picture had been posted all over the campus. There did not appear to be any trace of the girl. Her parents were alerted but had not seen her. George had interviewed most of the nurses in Patty's classes and none of them knew where she might be. He finally decided to visit Margie again. Her drove over to her dorm. It was already 4 PM; most classes should be over. It was almost the end of the semester and most of the student body was heading out for spring break. He walked up to Margie's room and knocked on her door. She answered the door and was shocked to see him.

"Did you find Patty?" she immediately asked.

"No…she is still missing." George entered her room. "Is it possible that she left for an early spring break?"

"No, all of her stuff is here and she would have told me if she was planning to do that."

"You told me that she always traveled in a group of students except when she went shopping. Where did she go shopping?" he asked.

"I don't know. She never told me which store she went to."

"Do you know if she used a credit card or paid cash?" he asked.

"I don't know, but she didn't have a credit card…at least I didn't ever see her use one when we were out somewhere. She always paid cash."

"She had to get cash somehow. Maybe she had a debit card," he said. "Can I look through her desk?"

"Go right ahead. It is the one by her bed there on the left." She pointed.

"Thanks." He rifled through the drawers but could not find any receipts or debit card records. It was possible that she had a debit card from her father and that it was in his name. He would have to check with the father. He turned back to Margie. "Do you know what she typically purchased when she went shopping?"

"It was typically fruit and snacks. She often shared them with me. I think there is still a bag of some snacks left over from last week on the shelf above the refrigerator," she recalled.

George walked over to the bag and opened it. There was an opened bag of pretzels and a small bag of chips in the bag. When he emptied the bag there was a small scrap of paper on the bottom. It was a $12.37 receipt from a store called Richardson's Stop and Shop. He grabbed the receipt and looked at Margie.

"Do you know where this store is?" he asked, showing her the receipt.

"No. not really. I typically get all my food in the cafeteria or in the Student Union."

"Well, if this is where she went on Wednesday, it might lead us to…" He stopped from saying her body, not wanting to upset Margie. "Well, I got to go. Thanks." He walked to the door. "She's dead isn't she?" Tears were running down Margie's cheeks.

"We don't know that," he said. He turned to leave. He got back to his car and called Andy Hall.

"Andy, do you know where Richardson's Stop and Shop is?" he asked. "Yeah, I think so. It is near the west side of the campus," Andy answered.

"Well, can you drive over to the Bennings dorm and meet me by the front door?" "Sure. I can get there in about ten minutes."

When Andy showed up, George asked him if he was going to walk to the Stop and Shop which way would he go? Andy started off walking to the west end of the campus. They eventually came to a path that led though a wooded area. Past the wooded area they saw the Stop and Shop. They went inside. They went over to the checkout counter. A young boy was just checking out a customer. He could not be much older than 16, but was working as a clerk. George waited until the customer left and he walked up to the boy. He was dressed in a store uniform, and the word 'Billy' was stenciled on his shirt.

"Billy?" George looked at him.

"Yes?" the boy was obviously shocked to see two policemen wanting to talk to him.

"Have you seen this girl?" George showed him a picture of Patty Sinclair.

"Yes…She comes in here about once a week. She is a very pretty girl. We often have a nice conversation… She typically buys fruit and potato chips." The boy was blushing slightly.

"So, she was here three days ago?" Andy asked.

"Yes, I think so. Why? Is something wrong?" Billy asked.

"Did you talk to her?" George asked.

"Yes we often talk about the weather. I have been trying to work up the nerve to ask her out but haven't yet." He looked at both officers. "What is wrong? Is she ok?"

"We can't say. She has gone missing and you may have been the last person to see her," George explained.

"Oh no…." The boy had heard about the killings on the campus.

"What is your full name and address?" Andy had his pencil and pad out.

"I'm Billy Wilson. I live over on Third street, 1346 Third street. I live with my parents."

"Ok. Thanks." Andy wrote it down. "What do you think?" he turned to George.

"I think we ought to go back." George started walking to the door, followed by Andy. When they were outside, George turned to Andy and said "We should look in those woods we passed."

CHAPTER 47

It was Sunday afternoon. Ron and Sue were at her dorm room. He was trying to help her with her Chemistry. Her final exam was on the last day of the semester. Sue was barely carrying a 'C' average but hoped to do well on the final. She was still having trouble balancing the chemical reactions. He tried to explain it to her but it just was not working for her. So, he made her repeat the same equation several times until she finally got it right. After several iterations she finally started to figure it out. She started to get some problems right on the first try.

"I think I understand it now." Sue smiled at Ron.

"You just had to iterate it a few times to get the solution," he agreed.

"Yeah, now I just do that in my head until I get the right answer."

"Hmmm…" he murmured.

"What?" She asked.

"I just got an idea how to maybe solve a problem at work." He smiled at her.

"Really? Helping me actually helped you?"

"Hey, sometimes it works that way," he explained.

"Well, I think I am ready for my test tomorrow," she said. "You want to go get something to eat?"

"Yeah that would be a good idea, where do you want to go?"

"I think that family restaurant over on Grant Street is open on Sundays, she replied.

Just then Joan, Sue's roommate entered. She did not look happy. "Have you guys heard?" she asked.

"Heard what?" Ron asked.

"I just saw Andy Hall just outside the dorm. He told me that they just found another body of a student yesterday over by the west woods near the campus. It looked like she had been raped and strangled." Joan looked down at the floor. It was obvious that she was upset.

"Oh no..." Sue moaned. "Not another one."

"I should go and talk to George," Ron put on his coat and walked to the door. "I will stop back before I leave for Cleveland tonight."

"OK," Sue said reluctantly.

Ron took a short walk over to the campus police department. As he got to the office he saw some unfamiliar faces wearing campus police uniforms. As he approached the office door, one of the new men stopped him. "What do you want? They are having a big meeting in there," he asked Ron.

"I wanted to see George." Ron held up his auxiliary police badge.

"Oh, you must be Pritchard?"

"Yeah, are you new?"

"I joined the force just last month. I remember seeing your name on the roster but never saw you around," the new officer explained.

"Well, I am only part time and spend most of my time in Cleveland now," Ron replied.

"I guess you can go in."

"Thanks." Ron entered the office. There were about eight people standing near George's desk. Ron recognized two of the campus police and George but the rest were unfamiliar. Two were dressed in suits and were probably city detectives. The rest wore city police uniforms.

"Hi George." George looked up and saw Ron. One of the detectives asked, "Who are you?"

"That's Ron Prichard, an auxiliary cop who helped me solve a rape case last summer," George explained.

"Well, we can use all the help we can get,'" the other detective said.

"I heard there was a third victim." Ron looked at Geroge.

"Yeah... forensics determined that she was electronically stunned, raped and then strangled. This time the killer's MO was a little different. She was tied to four trees with tape and not beaten like the first two. We still think it is the same guy. We will confirm this with a sample of his DNA," George explained. "The victim was a pretty nursing student who walked off campus in broad daylight and was attacked."

"Yeah, she was found inside the city limits so we have total jurisdiction on this one. We are still working with the campus police since she was a student," the first detective noted. "By the way where were you Wednesday afternoon?"

"I was working at my job in Cleveland," Ron responded.

"OK, we are checking everyone's alibi, I didn't mean anything for you."

"I'll vouch for Ron," George said. "I wish he worked for me full time, but he is working as an engineer in Cleveland."

The meeting continued with allocations of patrols and instituting a curfew for the campus. The city police would patrol the campus in cars, campus police would concentrate on foot patrols. Since the semester was over after tomorrow, the increased police presence would be put into place. If nothing else, they hoped it would discourage the killer from striking again. Ron stayed after the meeting broke up and the city police left.

"I wish I was here to help," Ron told George.

"Not much more you could do," George looked at him. "By the way, all three girls had the same physical form, height, hair color and eye color."

"Yes?" Ron was curious.

"Ron... I don't want to worry you, but they were all similar to your Sue."

"Oh my god," Ron exclaimed. "You think...?"

"It is probably just a coincidence, but you should maybe warn her to be extra cautious."

"I will." Ron had a frown on his face. He left to go back to Sue's dorm.

CHAPTER 48

R on had returned to work in Cleveland. He was back in the office. They had put him at the back of the office in a corner cubby so that he was basically hidden from the rest of the design group. He didn't mind since it reduced the distractions. He was still struggling with the pressure piston problem. He finally decided against trying to write a calculus formula for the it. There were just too many variables to consider. Instead, he was going to simulate a calculus problem by using a computer trick. He selected the physical dimensions of what he thought could be close and entered them into the basic computer program. When he ran it, it blew up and indicated an error since the changes were too difficult to calculate. He inserted a do-loop that compared the differential pressure and piston stroke 100 times a second. The program ran a little longer but still blew up. He then inserted a do-loop inside of the current do-loop that compared the pressures 100 times within each of the first 100 iterations. The program ran a bit longer but still stalled. He changed the internal do-loop from 100 to 1000 times. (In effect comparing the pressures and piston position 100,000 times a second.) This time the program ran to completion.

It did not provide the required correct final pressure or piston stroke, but now all he had to do was play with the physical dimensions until he got the correct design points. He was in the process of doing this when Penny came to his cubical.

"Hi Ron," she purred as she smiled at him. She was wearing a short green miniskirt, high heels and an almost transparent yellow blouse.

"Oh. Hello, Penny." He was surprised to see her again. God, she was sexy he thought.

"Would you be my hero and go get an old drawing out of the archives for me? I hate to ask any of the senior engineers."

"Uh…ok, sure" He didn't want to say no to such a pretty girl. "Where are the archives?"

"They are on the second floor. Here is the part number," she handed him a slip of paper.

"It will be a vellum so you need to run it through the blueprint machine." She smiled at him. She leaned over on his desk so he could see down the front of her blouse.

"Yeah, ok. Will do." He saved the program he was working on and got up to leave.

"Thanks." She replied as he worked past her, slightly brushing up against her breasts. She giggled.

"Sorry," he said as he headed toward the elevator. He had left his cell phone on his desk. She immediately picked it up and turned it on. He did not have a security code. This was going to be easy, she thought. She opened his contacts list and found the cell number for Sue Conner. She wrote it down, turned off his phone and replaced the phone where he had left it. Step one she thought to herself. She returned to her desk.

"Here you go," Ron said as he entered her office and handed her the rolled up print. He had been gone from his desk for 20 minutes.

"Thank you. You are a honey," she smiled sexily at him.

"Ok," Ron replied as he left the office and headed back to his cubical. He didn't think much of the task, but if a pretty girl asked him to do something he was not going to turn her down. Back at her desk, Penny threw the drawing into the paper shredder. She calculated that if it took him 20 minutes to find the old vellum, make a copy and replace the original in the file, she could make her plan work.

CHAPTER 49

*H*e *had narrowed his victim list down to one girl, the one he was obsessed with. He had been watching her from afar all of the time but now he really began to concentrate on her. She always seemed to be with a group of friends or with her boyfriend. He was going to have to think of a way to get close to her somehow. The first three victims were extremely satisfying but he needed to complete his obsession. It was literally driving him mad. No one suspected him yet but he knew the police were getting closer. If they stopped him and searched him and found a roll of tape and his stinger in his backpack he was doomed. They had started randomly searching the men on campus so he had hidden his gear in his apartment for now. Eventually he was stopped by a black policeman who did search him but did not find anything. It did shake him up though. If he'd had his equipment with him he would be in jail and a DNA match would have convicted him. So far they were not collecting DNA samples since these had to be given voluntarily. He did not doubt that eventually they would ask for volunteers to eliminate portions of the adult population from suspicion. He would need to act fast; time was running out.*

CHAPTER 50

Sue and Joan were back on campus; spring semester had started. Sue had only managed to pull a 'B' in chemistry but she was satisfied with that. Although both girls went home for the spring break, neither of them went partying down to Florida. Sue tried to exist at home with her brothers and stepfather. There were no significant pranks pulled on her for the week. Apparently her mother had laid down the law after the 'spill accident' at the restaurant. Joan had dropped her off at home but her mother drove her back to campus. Both her mother and stepfather were concerned about the 'Campus Strangler' and wanted her to skip a semester. She told them that she could not skip a semester since that would set her behind in her carefully planned scheduled career path and possible marriage.

She and Joan both had a requirement for an additional social studies class so they both picked basic Accounting. As they entered the class room Joan spied Greg Sommers sitting by himself, so she walked over and sat next to him. Sue followed and sat next to Joan.

"Hi Greg," Joan started.

"Oh, hello. What are you guys doing in this class? I thought this was for business students."

"Well, it is listed as a possible elective course for us also." Joan replied.

"Hi Greg," Sue said.

"Well, I guess it doesn't hurt to have a working knowledge of economics these days," Greg admitted.

"Yeah, with the campus strangler around Sue and I are taking as many classes together as we can," Joan exclaimed.

"God, I hope they catch that maniac soon," Greg agreed.

"He seems to be striking once a month," Joan said "I hope they find him before he gets another victim.

Sue was wondering about what Ron had told her about the victims and that they all tended to have her appearance. This scared her a bit but she was a third degree black belt and felt she could defend herself. Still, she was being extra careful not to go out alone anymore. She and Joan pretty much did everything together and typically stayed together as much as possible. If Joan had a date with Jerry, Sue simply stayed in her dorm room.

The Accounting class was starting so she shifted her thoughts to the class and the instructor who looked awful young to be a professor. The professor entered and scanned the room with his eyes. He had a very surprised look on his face when he saw the two pretty women sitting in his class. Typically, this was a class for first year business students which were predominately men. Wow. This might be an interesting semester after all he thought. The one young lady was breathtaking beautiful and he started thinking of how to get close to her.

CHAPTER 51

*I*cannot believe it. I have been stalking this girl for months… and now she shows up in my class. What are the odds of this happening? This may turn out to be quite an advantage. So far the police are clueless about who I am. The first three ladies were just appetizers. I fully intend to enjoy this girl, he thought to himself. Most of the pieces of his plan were falling into place. He just had to be patient a while longer. He wanted to fully possess her, not just have a quick encounter and then kill her like the other three. He wondered how long she would resist him before she submitted to him fully. It will be very interesting.

CHAPTER 52

Ron was at work. He had finally solved the problem with the pressure loading of the shock strut. He had sized the piston and the metering pin, adjusted the volumes and set the service pressures. When he ran the simulation, it gave the correct loading profile well within the stroke and size envelope available. He checked and re-checked his numbers. Everything was within limits. He decided to visit Lou Roberts and show him the digital printouts, sketch and data plots he had made from the data. He walked over to Lou's office. Penny was sitting at her desk.

"Hi Penny, is Lou in today?" Ron asked politely.

"Oh, hi Ron," she smiled at him. "I'll check to see if he is busy." She got up and walked to Lou's door. She was wearing a really short red mini skirt with a transparent white blouse that allowed the looker to see the outline of her strapless bra. Ron could not help but look at her and wonder how she would be in bed.

"Lou says he is not that busy, you can go on in," she purred at him with a smile on her face.

"Ok, Thanks." His face blushed slightly due to his impure thoughts. He went into the office. "Hello Ron. How is the design coming along?" Lou asked as he motioned for Ron to sit down.

"I think I have a solution," Ron stated as he started laying out the sketch and data plots on Lou's desk. Lou started looking at the data.

"Hey…This looks good. How did you do this in such a short time?" Lou scanned the data plots. "Do you have a calculus solution?"

"No…I simulated a calculus integration of the several variables using the computer program and then used it to size the components. As you can see, it meets the load profile and stroke and stays in the required envelope." Ron was blushing a bit.

"Well…I am impressed. Have a draftsman make the component drawings so we can order the parts as soon as possible. Then have Jeff order the necessary components to be made so we can test it."

"Can we test it here in our lab?" Ron asked.

"Yes. This is significantly smaller than the design Stan came up with. He has been trying to make a similar device work for months but has had no success. He has a rig already set up so we can have him test it. How do you intend to adjust it if it misses the target at test?"

"Well…I don't think we will need to adjust it …but I can have three different metering pins made up with slight variations in both directions," Ron explained.

"Excellent. Get right on it. By the way, what pressure exponent did you use for the mixed air/oil dynamic?" Lou was interested in the accuracy of the analysis.

"Well, I did a lot of research and decided on an exponent of 1.32 for the dynamic pressure input. It seems to work ok," Ron continued.

"That sounds about right. Let me know when you get it built and ready to test. I want to see it in action."

"Yes sir. I will do that," Ron agreed. He dreaded working with Stan Welland but there probably was no avoiding it. He got up and left the office. Penny smiled at him as he walked out. She had her chair turned toward him and had her legs open. Her skirt was so short, he could not help but see that she was exposing her black panties to him. He smiled at her but left in a hurry clutching his data sheets. He could not help but think that she was flirting with him even though he had told her that he was already engaged. Anyway, he would ponder that later. Right now, he was on a mission. He rushed over to Jeff Tyler's office and showed him the sketch and data sheets from the computer. Then he explained that Lou wanted the drawings made as soon as possible so that they could order prototype parts for a test. Jeff was impressed with the work he had done and smiled.

"Looks like you are making me look good for recommending you for the job. How did you solve the pressure stroke phenomena?" Jeff asked.

"I let the program calculate the changes, about a million times a second," Ron exclaimed.

"Wow. That is so cool. You really do have a bright future here." Jeff got up and walked over to the drafting section of the engineering office. He assigned the various parts to three different men and told them to drop what they were working on. He told them if they had any questions they were to ask Ron. Ron then sat down with them and started to explain how to read the dimensions from his data input sheet. Jeff quietly got up and walked back to his office. Along the way he stopped by Lou's office and walked right in. Penny did not bother even looking at him. "Hey Lou. Looks like the new kid has some good ideas," he said as Lou looked up.

"Yeah, I am impressed with him. I think he deserves a promotion and a raise to bring him up to the level of our other designers. I want him to stay and be happy here," Lou told Jeff.

"I was thinking the same thing. Glad we are on the same page," Jeff replied.

"Yeah, that kid is one smart cookie. And he doesn't brag about it either."

"I agree. He was really happy we are giving him a chance to work here." Jeff smiled.

"Just keep him happy," Lou ordered.

"Will do." Jeff left the office. Again, Penny ignored him. He wondered why she was so standoffish. She must have had a bad experience where she worked previously. She does excellent work but she sure could be more friendly. He knew almost every single guy in the engineering office had made a pass at her and gotten shot down. She wasn't friendly with the other women secretaries either so no one knew what her problem was. So now everyone had nicknamed her the 'Ice Maiden'. Even some of the sales and business guys from the third floor had tried to get to her and failed miserably. Oh well, not his problem. He already had a girlfriend and she was trying to push him toward matrimony. Still, he was interested in someone so beautiful but knew he did not have a chance with this one.

CHAPTER 53

George Coleman was about to pull out his hair. The campus strangler was still unknown. They now had his fingerprints from the tape he had used to tie up the third victim. They had sent these out to the FBI and Interpol hoping to find a match. So far nothing. They had his DNA, his fingerprints but he still was unknown. The city detectives were doing no better. They had checked for store cameras along the way to Richardsons Market but all they showed was the victim walking to and from the store. Her bag of groceries was found a few feet away from the girl, apparently where the killer had thrown it. There were no cameras along the path through the woods. The killer must have laid in wait in the woods and attacked her there. That indicated that he must have known that she would be walking that way. So, he determined that the killer must have stalked her for quite some time since according to the roommate she always traveled with a bunch of other nurses when she went to class on campus. So somehow the killer knew the one time that she would be alone in a relatively isolated area. Now that classes were back on for the spring semester, George was afraid that the killer would strike again. The killer's MO was slightly different this time since before he had killed the first two women someplace and then later dumped them. Apparently the increased police patrols had forced the killer to change his plans. The forensic people had found fibers from what apparently was a blanket that was under the victim but then later recovered by the killer. Also, the girl had not been beaten like the others. Maybe she had pleaded with him not to kill her if she cooperated. Still, she had been brutally raped with significant violence according to the autopsy report. There was evidence she had been gagged. Still, she was manually strangled the same as the other two women. George had originally wondered if it was possibly a copycat killing but he now knew it was the same killer. The girl had no boyfriend or anyone that was threatening her according to her parents or the roommate. So, either it was totally random or it was the killer of the first two. He knew that it was probably not random since she had been tasered as in the first two killings and had the same killer DNA in her body according to the Forensic lab. He was amazed that the killer did not seem to worry about leaving forensic evidence at the scene, almost daring the police to try to use it to find him. He must be arrogant and have a feeling of superiority over the police and obviously had little or no respect for the law or the police.

CHAPTER 54

APRIL

S ue and Joan were in the Accounting class. The subject matter was
not that difficult and Sue thought she understood the economic
principles. Supply and demand was pretty simple she thought. The
lectures by the professor were easy to follow but Sue had the feeling that
he was always looking directly at her and it made her feel uncomfortable.
Maybe it was just an illusion but he appeared to always have his eyes on
her. She didn't tell Joan about that but wondered if she should ask her
if it looked that way to her. She started to just listen and appear to be
writing in her notebook rather than meet his eyes. She knew that she
often attracted the looks of men on the campus but this seemed to be
so much more intense. She started to dress much more conservatively
on days she attended economic class. She started to wear her hair in
a ponytail and wore her glasses so that she looked not so attractive.
This had no effect on the man although Joan began to notice and
asked her why she dressed differently on Accounting class day. Sue did
not explain and just said she hadn't noticed dressing so differently on
those days. She knew that Joan did not believe her but she didn't care.
She had to continue the class since Joan would otherwise have to walk
by herself to class and they had promised each other to stick together
when on campus due to the killer. So, she simply concentrated on the
lessons and textbook while keeping her eyes averted from the professor
during his lectures. The information and coursework were easy enough

to understand even if the teacher was sort of creepy. She fully expected him to make a pass at her so she kept her engagement ring in plain sight all of the time. She felt that she should tell Ron about the situation but he might think she was imagining it. So, she stayed quiet about it and just tried to concentrate on her classwork.

CHAPTER 55

Ron was in his office, checking his numbers again. The prototype parts were due to arrive in a few days and he wanted to be sure he had made no mistakes on the numbers. He was totally absorbed when a hand touched his shoulder. He jumped, startled. It was Penny who had snuck up behind him.

"I'm sorry, I didn't mean to scare you," she said, concerned. She was wearing a green pants suit with a white blouse. Her makeup was perfect and she was as always very sexy looking.

"Uh…" He looked at her, "I am sorry I jumped, I was really concentrating on the final design stack up. What can I do for you?" he asked. He was again amazed at how beautiful and sexy she looked.

"I was wondering if you would do me a small favor again. He wants some of these old drawings from the archive and I don't know how to get them. Would you please be a dear and go down and get me a print of them?" she had a list of four drawings on a memo pad that she handed him.

"Ah…Sure, no problem." He got up from his desk, looking at the list. "This might take a while."

"It's no rush but I do need them as soon as possible." She purred with a sexy smile, her face only an inch from his. She smelled wonderful.

"I'll go right now." He got up and walked toward the elevator. He could not turn her down. She watched him get on the elevator and rushed back to his office. Again, he had left his cell phone on his desk. She grabbed it and made sure no one was looking. She walked down the hall to a corner office that was unoccupied. It was the one place in the building that had a window facing a cell tower and cell phones would work. She pulled out a special burner phone that she had paid a lot to a phone company guy to give it a number that was one digit different from Sue's phone. She turned on his phone and went to his contacts list. Sue's number was at the top. She edited the number by one digit so it would ring the burner phone she had. Most people did not memorize the phone numbers but simply pressed the contact button to make a call. With any luck Ron would not notice that the number had changed by one digit. She then transferred a message onto his phone. It read: 'DEAR SUE: I AM SORRY THAT I MUST BREAK OFF OUR ENGAGEMENT. I HAVE MET ANOTHER WOMAN THAT I HAVE FALLEN IN LOVE WITH. PLEASE UNDERSTAND THAT I CANNOT ACCEPT YOUR CALLS ANY LONGER. YOU MAY KEEP THE ENGAGEMENT RING IF YOU WANT. I HAVE INCLUDED A PHOTO OF HER. GOOD BYE.' She copied a picture she had taken in her bedroom of herself naked from the waste up, smiling at the camera onto the message. Then she set his phone to block Sue's old real number if Sue called Ron. Then Penny sent the message with the picture to Sue. After she was sure it was sent, she deleted the message so Ron would never see it. So now, any calls he made to Sue would show up on the burner phone Penny had, and any calls Sue made to Ron would be blocked. She smiled. This was just too easy, she thought. She walked back to Ron's desk and replaced his phone on his desk. She went back to her office and turned off the burner phone. After he had returned with the prints, Penny thanked him with a smile and he went back to his desk. She then shredded the prints in the paper shredder. When he was sure that he had returned to his desk, she went to the corner office again, turned on the burner phone and texted Ron what he would think was from Sue. 'Ron: I AM CALLING OFF OUR ENGAGEMENT; I HAVE MET ANOTHER MAN THAT I HAVE FALLEN IN LOVE WITH. I AM SORRY

THAT THIS HAS TURNED OUT THIS WAY BUT IT IS FOR THE BETTER. I KNOW THAT YOU WILL PROBABLY MEET ANOTHER WOMAN THAT MEETS YOUR NEEDS BETTER. PLEASE DO NOT CALL ME OR VISIT ME ANYMORE. SUE.' She sent the text to Ron. He would not get it until he left the building but that was ok. She would make sure that she would be available to comfort him in his lost love.

Ron had learned that the parts were in the test lab and Jeff Tyler wanted him to assemble the shock strut tomorrow morning and prepare to test it. He noted that Lou wanted to see the test. Ron agreed to the request but now it was time to go home. Ron walked out of the office building at quitting time. His phone immediately binged, letting him know that he had a text message. He ignored it until he got into the shade of the building. Then he opened the message. It was from Sue. He read the message and was in a state of shock. The woman he intended to spend his life with had now rejected him. He immediately tried to call her but it went to voice mail. Instead of her normal message, it had a mechanical voice saying to leave a message. He was somewhat confused by this but left her a message to call him as soon as possible. He involuntary sat down as tears streamed down his face. He was careful not to let the other employees see him as they were leaving the plant. He staggered to his feet and started walking to his apartment two blocks away. He could not believe Sue would do this to him after they had discussed their future plans in such detail. He felt as if someone had punched him hard in the stomach. Why? he asked himself. How could Sue, his Sue, be so cruel to him? Had he missed something in their relationship? He thought that she loved him. He got to his apartment and sat on his bed. He knew that he needed to drive down to the campus to see her, but he had the test to set up tomorrow morning. As soon as the test was over he would drive to the campus and confront her. Then his phone binged again. It said it was from Sue (but was actually being sent by Penny). 'RON. I UNDERSTAND YOU MAY BE UPSET BUT PLEASE DO NOT TRY TO SEE ME

OR CALL ME AGAIN. WE ARE THROUGH.' Ron was shocked by the blunt rejection. Had he been so blinded by love that he had not seen this type of attitude in her personality? He had told her that he would be faithful to her no matter what. She had answered that she would keep the engagement ring forever unless he asked her to return it. His attitude hardened. If that was the way she wanted it, he would honor her wishes. He texted back 'OK. I LOVE YOU - BUT IF THIS IS WHAT YOU WANT, SO BE IT. GOOD BYE.' He rolled over and went into a troubled sleep. (The message did not go to Sue but to Penny's burner phone).

Sue Conner was in her dorm room and laying on her bed crying her eyes out. Joan entered and was shocked to see her roommate obviously distraught.

"What is the matter?" she asked carefully as she put her hand on Sue's back.

"He…he…Ron…" Sue could not finish the sentence she was crying so hard, but shoved her cell phone over to Joan so she read the message. Joan read the message but was shocked that Ron would do this to her friend. He and Sue were so obviously deeply in love that Joan figured that nothing would ever come between them. Now there was a naked picture of a sexy woman that had obviously seduced Ron. She could not believe that she had misjudged Ron so bad. He had completely fooled her that he was deeply and entirely committed to her roommate. The message did not sound like Ron at all. She took Sue's phone and texted Ron: 'RON, HOW CAN YOU DO THIS TO SUE? SHE IS COMPLETELY IN LOVE WITH YOU. – JOAN. She sent it - but got a message back saying that it was blocked at the other end. Wow, this is really bad. She thought. She tried to console Sue but to no avail. Ron must be a real bastard Joan thought.

CHAPTER 56

Ron was in the test lab. He had assembled the shock strut but did not have his heart in the work. He was still upset by the breakup with Sue. Now he had to work with Stan Welland who obviously hated him with a passion. Ron had to watch the setup carefully in case Stan sabotaged the test. Once everything was ready, Jeff Tyler and Lou Roberts entered the lab and walked over to the test setup. They wanted to see if the young engineer had actually solved the problem. Everyone went into the block house near the setup and watched as Gary Ault did a final check on the instrumentation. Once he gave the thumbs up and entered the block house he turned on the computer and the data recorder. As everyone looked through the window, Stan engaged the test. The test fired and they heard the data recorder spit out the results at one reading per millisecond. The test was over and Stan walked over to the data sheet. He fully expected it to be a failure. Ron's prototype was much smaller than the one he had designed and had been testing for several months without success.

"This can't be right," Stan said as he looked at the data. The test results were well within the design parameters.

"Let me see," Lou asked as he looked at Stan. Stan gave him the readout. "Well, it looks like we have a winner here." Lou smiled.

"I must have messed up the test trigger," Stan said.

"OK, let's run it again to confirm the numbers," Jeff Tyler said.

"Yeah, let's do it again," Stan agreed. He could not understand how the kid engineer could possibly get it right on the first shot without any iterations. It just was not possible. They reset up the test and ran the test again. The results were identical within experimental error.

"Looks good to me," Jeff replied as he read the data.

"Good." Lou slapped Ron on the back. "Now you get to go to Edwards Air Force Base to run the test on an actual test aircraft." He spoke to Ron. "Are you ok with that?" he asked.

"I guess so," Ron replied meekly. He was still numb from losing the love of his life. It did not matter now if he returned to the campus on the weekends now. He resigned himself to traveling to California for the aircraft tests.

"Good, good." Lou smiled. He was getting to really like Ron. This kid was amazing, he thought.

Stan was standing in the corner. He could not believe what he had seen. He had worked on this problem for several months without success and the new kid comes up with the correct solution in only three weeks. The kid must be really smart. He wondered how he could get even with the kid. Trouble was that Ron now had Lou as a protector and would mentor him. All his years working in the test lab to become the senior lab test engineer were now threatened. This was the second time that Ron had made him look bad. It did not look as if Lou paid any attention to him right now, but he had to wonder if his job was in jeopardy.

CHAPTER 56

S ue Conner sat in her dorm room talking to Joan, her roommate.

"How could he do this to me?" she asked Joan. The phone message from Ron had been a terrible shock to her. She was having a hard time dealing with it.

"I don't understand it," Joan answered. "I thought he was head over heels in love with you. That just doesn't sound like something Ron would do."

"I need to talk to him. I need to know why." Sue had cried for hours and was all cried out. She reached for her phone.

"I tried to call him on your phone but it was blocked at the other end," Joan replied.

"Why would he do that?" Sue asked, and tried dialing Ron again but got the same message saying that the call was blocked. Her entire life was now in turmoil. All the plans that she and Ron had made were now washed away. She was confused. Was her father really right about long distance relationships not working? She looked at the engagement ring on her finger. She took it off and threw it against the far wall. Joan walked over and picked it up and handed it back to her.

"I think you should return this to him and ask why he did this to you," Joan insisted.

"What if he won't even see me?"

"I doubt that he is that cruel. He always impressed me that he was a sensitive, caring person," Joan remembered. "This whole thing doesn't seem to be like him at all."

"I know. That is one of the reasons I fell in love with him." Sue started to cry again.

"We need to confirm that Ron actually feels this way and find out who this woman is that has turned him against you," Joan replied. "What if he didn't send the message?"

"What do you mean?" Sue stopped crying.

"Well, this impersonal termination of the relationship is so unlike Ron, I cannot help but wonder if someone got hold of his phone and sent it," Joan theorized. "I doubt that he would send a naked picture of anyone in a message. Either that, or I really misjudged him to be more of a gentleman than he really is. I am pretty sure that he would have told you in person, or he really badly fooled us."

"You may be right. I need to confirm this." Sue had a glimmer of hope.

CHAPTER 57

MAY

Ron was in his Cleveland apartment packing up his things to take to California. He would probably have to be there for a couple of weeks. Without thinking he pulled his phone out and dialed Sue. It went straight to voice mail. He left a message saying that he just had to talk to her and would she meet with him? A few minutes later he got a text message from (Penny) her. 'THERE IS NO REASON TO TALK. WE HAVE NOTHING TO SAY TO EACH OTHER. GOODBYE.' Ron was devastated. Sue wouldn't even let him ask what he had done to make her forget his love for her. Who was the guy she was in love with? How could everything change in such a short time? Was she just leading him on all this time? It sure did not sound like Sue. When they made love she was very passionate with him and kept saying that they would be together for all time and that her love for him would never stop. Something must have happened. He must have offended her in such a way that she wanted out of the relationship. He thought hard but could not think of what he did or said to offend her. He had to find out. He dialed George Coleman, his best friend.

"George, how are you doing?" Ron asked intently. "I need to talk to you."

"Hi Ron…hey, I can't talk right now I am in a meeting with the state police and the FBI." He hung up.

"Wow," Ron said as he put his phone away. No one wants to talk to me. He started to feel a little depressed. He walked out of the apartment and stored his stuff in his car. He drove to work even though it was only two blocks away.

Ron was at his desk cleaning up a few odds and ends. Penny came into his office.

"Hello Ron. The prototype parts were shipped to Edward's AFB. I have your airline tickets to LAX and your pass to get on base." She handed him a manilla envelope. "Are you all right? You look sad," she said, concerned.

"Oh, hi Penny. My girlfriend just broke up with me and I don't know why." Ron looked at her with a tired look. He had not gotten much sleep.

"Oh…I am so sorry." She said in low voice, putting her hand on his. "If there is anything I can do…" she purred.

"I guess I just don't understand women," he said looking at the floor.

"Well…you better get going. You have a plane to catch," she said, rubbing his shoulder. She leaned toward him for a kiss but he did not notice.

"Yeah, thanks." He got up.

She stood in his way, facing him. "When you get back maybe we can do something about that," she said.

"I don't know…" he said, still looking at the floor.

Later, Ron was in a 737 aircraft winging to Los Angeles. George tried to call him but could not get through since Ron had switched his cell phone off. George was puzzled since Ron had seemed to be very intent on talking to him. Oh well, maybe it was not that important after all.

Sue and Joan had decided to try to call Ron at work, bypassing his cell phone and getting through to him through the switchboard. They dialed the company main line.

"Hello, Newmatic Company." The operator answered.

"Hello, I am trying to reach an employee named Ron Pritchard," Sue said, excitedly.

"Do you know what department he is in or his extension?" the operator asked.

"I don't have his extension but I know he is in engineering. This is an emergency," Sue lied.

"Ok…" The operator hesitated. "I will connect you to engineering." She called the engineering secretary and relayed the message that a woman wanted to talk to a Ron Pritchard and that it was an emergency.

"I will take the call." Penny told the operator. The operator connected them.

"Hello. This is engineering," Penny started. "What is this about?"

"Hello…I must speak to Ron Pritchard; it is very important," Sue responded.

"Can I ask who is calling?" Penny was suspicious.

"I am Sue Conner. I need to talk to Ron…please let me talk to him?" Sue pleaded.

"Is this about the wedding?" Penny asked. She started to think fast.

"What wedding?" Sue was puzzled.

"Oh…he is getting married next month, that is why he is out of the office today."

"Who is he getting married to?" Sue asked desperately.

"I believe it is a co-worker he met here at work, why do you ask?" Penny answered.

"Oh…" Sue hung up.

"What did she say" Joan asked.

"Ron is getting married." Sue collapsed, crying again. "To a co-worker," she sobbed.

"That bastard," Joan replied.

Penny grinned after Sue hung up. That should take care of the fiancée for good she figured. Her plan was working out perfectly. Now Ron wouldn't have any reason to contact Sue and if he tried it would be to get a very cold reception. She called her brother to give him the good news.

CHAPTER 58

MAY

S ue and Joan were in the Accounting class. Joan was sitting next to Greg Sommers and Sue was sitting next to Joan. The class had not started yet as the instructor was late. Greg looked over at Sue and whispered to Joan, "What is wrong with Sue? She looks like she is depressed or something."

"She has been dumped by her fiancé," Joan whispered back.

"Oh…I am sorry to hear that," he whispered.

"Yeah, the bastard didn't even have the guts to tell her to her face."

"That seems awful cruel," he said sympathetically.

Just then the instructor came into the classroom. He took off his coat and hung it on his chair and opened his brief case. "I am sorry I am late. I was delayed by a very important call." He stood facing the class. "I have decided to give a 'Snap Quiz'" as he handed out test sheets. "This is a closed book exam and please do not use your cell phones." He looked at Sue and noted that she did not look as pretty as she typically did. She was still beautiful but looked very sad. Oh well, he thought, not everyone liked a surprise test.

After class Sue, Joan and Greg walked out of class together. "You guys want to go to the student union and get a snack? I'll treat" Greg tried to cheer them up.

"That test was awful." Joan groaned.

"You guys go along...I don't feel like a snack" Sue replied. She also thought the test was bad. She had not been studying as she typically did. Her mind was elsewhere. She knew she had probably failed the test which was very unlike her. She turned around and re-entered the classroom. Greg and Joan kept walking away talking to each other. The instructor was walking out of the classroom and almost collided with Sue.

"Sorry," he said as he stopped.

"Can I ask about extra credit?" I don't think I did very well on that test," Sue asked.

"Ah...ok, come to my office and we will talk about it," he said smiling at her. He turned off the lights and they walked to his office.

"Where is Sue?" Joan turned around looking for her friend. "I thought she was right behind us."

"I thought she was with us too." Greg had a troubled look on his face. "Should we go back and look for her?" he asked.

"We probably should." She turned around and walked back to class. Greg followed her. They got to the classroom but it was dark and no sign of Sue.

"Where do you suppose she got to?" Greg asked. "It's not a good idea for girls to walk around by themselves with a killer on the loose," he whispered, half afraid that something had happened to Sue.

"I don't know, but I am starting to get worried," Joan replied.

CHAPTER 59

Ron had landed at LAX and rented a car to take him to Edwards Air Force Base. He was wearing his basic khaki pants, white shirt and blue blazer. Although it was only May, the temperature was in the eighties and sunny. It was early in the morning and he was glad that he had eaten a snack in the airport. He left the airport and traveled north on Interstate Route 15. He then turned off onto Route 395 North which took him to Mesquite Canyon Road which took him south to the Air Force Base. Pulling up to the guard post he showed the guard his ID and gate pass. He had to go inside of the guard post to fill out some paperwork and was then told which building to go to. He was warned to stay away from a couple of buildings which were under high security. He finally found the right building and went inside where he had to show his ID and pass again to the Sargent manning the desk. He was told to enter an adjacent room and wait for the officer in charge. There were other men sitting in the room. One man wearing a gray suite came up to him and asked if he was the engineer from Newmatic. He responded yes, that he was here to witness a test of his shock strut. The man said he had reviewed the design and thought it was too small to do the job. Ron responded that he was told that it had to fit in the envelope so he designed it to fit. The man shook his head and walked away. Ron wondered who he was and how he had seen the design. Finally, a man wearing a blue Major's uniform came in and greeted Ron. He escorted Ron and the man in the gray suite into a large hanger room with an aircraft parked in it. They walked to the other side of the hanger and had a meeting in an office with a bunch of other Air Force personnel. It turned out that the man in the gray suit was a representative of the aircraft airframe maker and he started the meeting by telling the Air Force people that the shock strut was to small and would not support the airframe. Much discussion followed and the Major turned to Ron and asked him to support his design. Ron opened his brief case and handed out the test results from the testing done in his lab. He went on to explain the workings of the mechanism and provided a load stroke curve that showed that it could support the specified load. Again, much discussion followed but in the end the consensus was to go forward with the test of the shock strut on the following day. Ron left the meeting and drove out of the base to the hotel the company had reserved for him. After checking in at the hotel, he noticed an outdoor pool that no one was using. He changed into swim trunks and headed to the pool. The water was warm, almost too warm and the sun was beating down. He realized that if he stayed in the pool too long he would get a terrible sunburn so he got out and dried off. That was probably why no one else was in the pool at this time of the day. He went back to his room and laid on the bed. All morning he had not been thinking of his break up with Sue but had concentrated on the presentation to the Air Force. Now it hit him again. Why would she break his heart like this with no explanation? He decided to call her again but again it went straight to voice mail. He left a message.

"Please Sue, can you at least tell me why you want to break up? I think I at least deserve that." He hung up. A few minutes later he got an email: SORRY RON, BUT I AM IN LOVE WITH ANOTHER MAN. PLEASE TRY TO FORGET ME. (It was from the burner phone that Penny was using but showed up on his phone as from 'Sue'.)

Again, he was devastated. She refused to talk to him and it hurt deeply. Still, if she wanted to be left alone, he would not continue to bother her. He still did not understand but he would never force himself on any girl. He had told her that she could leave the relationship if she wanted to and apparently she wanted to. There was no reason now to keep the apartment on campus. When he got back to Cleveland he would find a larger apartment than the small efficiency he currently had at work and move his belongings from the college to the new apartment. He had nothing back on campus but his friend George and he was busy with the problems on campus. Ron wondered if they had caught the killer yet. He hoped so.

CHAPTER 60

George was in his police station on campus. He had a meeting with the city detectives and the FBI. The FBI got pulled into the case by the city police who needed help with the case. Since the victims were all apparently 'kidnapped' prior to being killed, technically they could try to help out. George did not quite like the FBI attitude towards his 'hick' campus police force but could tolerate it if they helped to solve the case. At least they were letting him attend the strategy meetings with the city police. The plans had not changed much. Increased police patrols and video surveillance had not yet revealed anything. The bad part of this is the killer probably would strike again and they had to hope that he would make a mistake. Since December the killings were all about six weeks apart and it was almost six weeks from the last victim's death. He was actually anticipating the next victim. So far all of the victims had been campus students. There had not been any similar such attacks in the city next to the campus. The DNA evidence found on the victims pointed to a lone wolf who didn't have a partner. Or at least there was no evidence to indicate that anyone was helping him. His officers had stopped and searched some students that had bulging backpacks or acted suspicious. This was stopped since the students started to complain to the Dean of the campus. George now had a total of six regular officers besides himself and they worked in shifts patrolling the campus. Also, the city police had two patrol cars assigned to drive around campus trying to notice any irregularities. The student body were all nervous and a lot of parties had been canceled. Most of the students, especially the women pretty much just went to class and stayed in their dorms at night. There were a few brave souls that went to the bars bordering the campus but they would always travel in groups, feeling there was safety in numbers. George didn't know what else to do. All of the suggestions made by the FBI were already in place. A couple of FBI agents went undercover and started attending classes. They stood out like sore thumbs and the students knew they were police, but were actually happy to have them around. George tried to patrol as much as possible himself, concentrating mostly around the Student Union since two of the victims had made contact with the killer there. He was not spending much time with his fiancée Jennifer, but she understood the situation and knew he was under a lot of pressure.

CHAPTER 61

Greg Sommers had escorted Joan back to her dorm safely. Sue was not in the room. Greg said he would go over to the police department to report Sue missing unless Joan called him if Sue returned. She agreed but sat down worrying. Why would Sue go off by herself? Joan knew that Sue had a black belt in Karate and was confident she could fight off any aggressor, but these days, it was better to stay together. She called her boyfriend Jerry just to talk to someone. Jerry was a junior at the college and a member of a fraternity but still needed two more years to graduate. He had decided to get a degree in social science but living at the fraternity house was difficult since there were a lot of distractions that made it hard to study. Jerry was only carrying a 2.0 average but he was trying harder now that he thought he had a future with Joan. She explained to him that Sue did not return with her from Accounting class and that she was worried. Jerry tried to reassure her that Sue was pretty smart and would not let herself get into a bad situation. He asked her if she wanted him to come over but she said no, she would call him later.

Joan knew that Sue had broken up with Ron although she did not understand why Ron had treated her so badly. Joan figured if ever there were two people more in love than Ron and Sue, she had not seen it before. That is why it was so puzzling to her that he was so impersonal to her. Ever since the breakup Sue had been walking around as if in a trance, so Joan was not sure that Sue was being very careful about being alone on campus. When Sue did not show up after an hour, Joan began to really get nervous. Where was she? She almost called the police but didn't yet. They wouldn't act on anything unless a person was missing for 48 hours. Joan thought that might be too late but she decided to wait. She almost put on her jacket to go out to look for Sue but hesitated since she didn't want to be a victim. She huddled on her bed in a fetal position, scared for Sue.

CHAPTER 62

*H*e was just about ready to spring his trap on his primary victim. She really looked depressed since she had broken up with her boyfriend. She would be much more accessible now and apparently much easier without her normal confident attitude. He licked his lips at the thought of getting her. He would abduct her and the stupid police would wait 48 hours and then start to look for her body. He had a much different scenario in mind this time and they would be wasting their time looking for her. He would carry out his plan. This one girl was the one he was obsessed with and he wanted to completely possess her. He knew she would resist him at first like the others but that always changed. When they knew or thought they were going to die, they changed their attitude. It did not help them in the end, however. He prepared his equipment for the event. The stinger was all charged up. In the end she would beg him but it would not help. He could not wait.

CHAPTER 63

Ron was at the test hanger. The aircraft was all ready to go. There had been much discussion on his device but in the end the pilot agreed to run the test. They all watched as the aircraft taxied out on the runway and took off into the air. The aircraft was heavily loaded with a maximum weapons load (all were deactivated for the test). The aircraft came in for a landing and had no problems. The test was a success. So, Ron was elated and felt happy that his part had performed as expected. The Air Force Major came over and congratulated him, saying the test results recorded by the instrumented aircraft basically matched what his predicted data was exactly. Ron called his office to let Lou know that the test was successful. Lou was happy and told him that he was going to get a raise. Normally this would have made Ron happy but now he had no reason to accumulate any wealth since he did not have a future wife to support. He mumbled thanks and terminated the call. He would have to stay for a couple of days to review the test data with the Air Force engineers, but it looked as if his company would now win the contract. It turned out that the airframe company had an item to test also but admitted that they could not meet the maximum specified load so their device was not tested. Ron's shock strut met the maximum load condition and even showed some margin. The Air Force people were very excited. The Major walked over to Ron.

"I understand you designed this shock strut?" he asked.

"Yes. I worked it out on a computer model and eventually was able to adjust the design to meet the requirements," Ron explained.

"Have you ever thought about working as an independent civilian contractor for the Air Force? the Major asked.

"Ah, no… I just started working for Newmatic and don't have a lot of experience," Ron responded.

"Well, if you ever want to join us, please contact me." He handed Ron his card. "We have some very nice benefits and the weather here in southern California is probably a lot nicer than Cleveland," the Major smiled. Ron was shocked. He had worked hard to get the computer program to design the parts but he felt that he had just been lucky to figure out the solution. He knew if he joined these people they would expect him to provide the same level of expertise as this time and he knew he was not experienced enough to be able to provide that. He was already wondering what was the next project they would throw at him at work. Every time he had started a new project, he learned something. He needed to learn a lot more before he could think about going somewhere else.

CHAPTER 64

Joan was sitting on her bed in her dorm room wondering where Sue was. It was not like Sue to not let Joan know where she was. She had been missing almost three hours. It was starting to get dark outside. Joan tried calling her but it went right to voicemail. So, she was starting to get worried. Just then the door opened and Sue walked in.

"Hello! Where did you go after class?" Joan said, relieved to see her.

"Oh hi. I did so bad on that exam that I stayed to talk to the professor about extra credit.

He was heading out to get a coffee so he invited me to join him. He drove us to a coffee house just off campus."

"You don't drink coffee."

"Yeah but they do have some herbal teas so I had one of those. Then he explained to me what type of term paper I could write to improve my grade. Afterward he drove me back to our dorm," Sue explained.

"So… you had a 'date' with our instructor?" Joan asked.

"It wasn't a date. We just discussed the extra credit paper."

"It sure sounds like date to me," Joan grinned.

"The funny thing is…he drove me right to our dorm and I didn't even tell him which dorm I was in…that seemed strange," Sue said.

"You must have mentioned it; maybe you don't remember." Joan walked over to the door and locked it. "Anyway, Greg and I were worried about you running around campus alone with a killer on the loose."

"I am sorry, I tried to call you but my phone died." I have been so depressed about the breakup that I must have forgotten to charge it."

"Well don't let it happen again. You don't know when you might need to call 911." Joan climbed into bed.

"You forget I have a third degree black belt in Karate?" Sue asked.

"That won't help you if you get attacked from behind."

"We are trained to react when caught off guard. So don't worry about me. If the guy attacks me he will get a real surprise." Sue started to get ready for bed.

CHAPTER 65

Ron had to stay the rest of the week at Edwards Air Force Base to review the test data and meet with the program manager on the product to discuss the program follow up testing. Although the first test item was just a prototype, Ron explained that it could go into production fairly quickly. After the final conference Ron prepared to leave the base. As he got into his rental car he started to think about Sue again. It was easy to forget about her when he was concentrating on his project and attending meetings. Now that it was all over, his mind took him back to his lost love. He decided that he was definitely going to visit campus and confront Sue. She would have to explain why she could not even tell him face to face that she was not in love with him anymore. It might hurt him a lot but he had to know. They had been through a lot together and he felt he deserved to know who the person was that she was now in love with. He wouldn't call her to warn that he was coming. He would just show up and play it by ear. He caught his flight back to Cleveland and thought about the campus killer. He wondered if George had caught the man yet. He had not talked with George for several weeks. Ron was still an auxiliary police officer but had not touched base with the department since the killings had started. He decided he should call George once he got back to Cleveland.

CHAPTER 66

It was getting close to the end of the spring Semester. Sue had written a term paper and turned it in to the Accounting Professor. It was only 2 days to the final exam. Greg, Joan and Sue were in the Accounting classroom listening to the last lecture of the semester. As the class ended, Greg and Joan walked out into the Hall, followed by Sue. Greg was talking intently to Joan.

"I thought you were dating Sally?" Joan was saying to Greg.

"I was but she is not available. I really wanted to go to this concert. The seat tickets cost $50 each. Are you sure you can't make it?" he pleaded with Joan.

"I already have plans with Jerry…He would be devastated if I changed plans now." She held her hands out at her sides.

"Ok, I am sorry. I guess I will just not go. I hate to go to something like this without a date to talk to." He was frowning, looking at the floor.

"How about Sue? She isn't engaged anymore," Joan turned to Sue.

"What?" Sue asked. She had only caught the end of the conversation.

"I know you are upset about your recent breakup…but would you like to go to the orchestra concert tomorrow? Sally cancelled out on me." Greg looked hopeful. Sue thought about it. Why not? She had been living like a hermit, suffering in silence ever since the breakup.

"Yeah. I guess I could go." She had dated Greg a couple of times in high school but they had never really hit it off. "What time do you want to pick me up?" Sue asked.

"Well, it starts at 8. How about I come to get you at 7:15?"

"Sounds good." She smiled at him.

They walked to the student union where they all had hot chocolate and donuts. Greg was smiling at Sue and she was beginning to feel human again. It would be nice to start living again, she thought. Greg was not really her type of guy but the concert should be enjoyable. It was entirely possible that he had changed and matured since high school. She certainly hoped so. She started to think about what she should wear to a concert. She was not really into classical music but it was Rachmaninov and she had heard the second concerto once with Ron and it was very good. She was looking forward to a nice night out.

CHAPTER 67

Ron was back in Cleveland. It was late afternoon and he decided not to go back to work. Instead, he decided to go to his efficiency apartment and crash for the night. He would skip work tomorrow and drive to the campus in southern Ohio to confront Sue. He got to his apartment and took a shower. He was tired from the jet lag so he took a small nap. Later, after unpacking, he decided to call George.

"George?" he asked.

"Hello." George was on the other end.

"How's things going on the campus.?"

"Ron? Is that Ron, the famous engineer?" George kidded.

"Yes, but not famous...yet," Ron laughed. "Have you caught the bad guy yet?"

"No, we are still working the case. It has been a tough semester."

"I am sorry I haven't been there for you. I had to go to California for a test program at Edwards Air Force Base."

"Sounds like you have been busy," George commiserated. "By the way, I ran into Joan the other day and she said that you had broken up with Sue. What the heck is going on? I thought you guys were deeply in love."

"I didn't cause the breakup...she told me she had met another guy and was in love with him," Ron declared.

"That's not what I heard. Joan said she saw a text message from you that said you had met another woman and was in love with her. It just about destroyed Sue," George replied.

"I never sent a message like that. And by the way, it's not true, I am still in love with Sue but I got text messages from her saying she wanted to break off the engagement." Ron was getting angry.

"Wait a minute, you mean you were acting on a text message, you didn't even have the balls to tell her in person?" George was getting angry.

"Yeah, when I tried to call her it went straight to voicemail and she would text me back saying to leave her alone...not call me."

"Hold on...so you didn't actually talk to her?" George replied. "Because Sue has been hiding in her room mourning the end of the relationship. Joan says she thinks you're a bastard for breaking up with Sue with a text message."

"I did not send her any such message." Ron was getting confused.

"It sounds as if someone is trying to break you guys up and hacked into your phones." George was getting concerned.

"I need to get down there tomorrow to try to straighten this out." Ron had a glimmer of hope for the relationship.

"That sounds like a good idea. Maybe I will go over to see Sue in the morning and tell her that someone is playing a trick on you guys," George suggested.

"Yeah, tell her I never sent that message." Ron hung up. Maybe this was just all a misunderstanding. He checked his phone messages. There was no record of sending anything like that. He checked Sue's number. His eyes lit up. The number was incorrect! It was one digit off from what he knew her number was. He dialed the false number for Sue. There was no answer. It went to voice mail. He said into the phone "*Who are you and why are you doing this?*" A few minutes later a text message reply showed up. "You are *too late now. It is in progress.*"

Ron was puzzled by the response. What was in progress? Then he began to worry. What did this have to do with his relationship with Sue? He hurriedly called George back.

"George, can you check with Sue to see if she is ok? I just got a strange message."

"Gee Ron, it is getting late. Can it wait until morning?"

"No. Please go and check to see if she is ok...please?" Ron pleaded.

"Ok...I'll go over to her dorm to check." George was puzzled.

"Thanks, I am going to drive down there now." Ron hung up. He then tried to call Sue on the number he knew was her actual number. Sue looked at her phone and saw it was Ron calling. She couldn't stand anymore rejection messages from him so she killed the call. He was getting desperate so he left her a text message: *'Sue: I didn't send the message to you about breaking up. I think we have been hacked. I am driving down to see you tonight. I love you, Ron.'*

Sue saw a message come in on her phone but ignored it for now since she was walking down stairs to meet Greg.

CHAPTER 68

George drove over to Sue and Joan's dormitory. He could tell from Ron's call that he was upset. He wondered what this was all about. He parked his patrol car in the lot and walked over to the building. He had visited Sue once or twice before with Ron so he thought he remembered her room. It was on the third floor he thought. He walked up to her door and knocked. Joan opened the door. Joan's plans with Jerry had changed due to a fraternity thing.

"Hello George, what brings you out tonight?" Joan asked, surprised to see the campus police chief at her door.

"Hi Joan. Can I talk to Sue?" George asked.

"She isn't here, she left about fifteen minutes ago. Why, what's wrong?"

"I got a call from Ron Pritchard...He says he never sent Sue a text message about breaking up."

"That bastard...wait, he never sent it? It came from his phone. When we tried to call his office, the secretary said he was out of town preparing for his marriage ceremony to a co- worker." Joan frowned.

"He was out of town all right, he had to go to California for some test for work," George explained. He said he got a text message from Sue saying that she wanted to break off the engagement."

"Sue never would do that; she was totally in love with Ron. She was devastated when she got his text message." Joan was puzzled.

"This sounds like a conspiracy. It appears that someone hacked into their phones and sent false messages," George theorized.

"Why would someone want to break them up? Anybody could tell that they were deeply in love," Joan noted. "Maybe it was that secretary where he works. Maybe she is trying to steal Ron away from Sue?"

"Could be. Anyway, he is driving down tonight to see her. Where did she go?" George asked.

"She was feeling so down but wanted to get out and live a little. When Greg asked her to go to a concert with him she said Ok," Joan explained.

"Who is this Greg?" George was getting suspicious.

"Oh…He is an old friend from high school. He graduated with us and is in a couple of classes with me and Sue. His name is Greg Sommers. He dated Sue in high school a couple of times."

"You said they went to a concert? On a weekday?" George asked.

"Well, the semester is almost over and we have almost finished all of our classes, so why not?"

"Can you call her? Tell her to get back here? I don't have her number in my phone."

"I suppose I could, but can't it wait until morning? Sue was really looking forward to this concert." Joan looked at George and saw he was worried. "Ok, I will call her now." She got her cell phone and dialed Sue's number. There was no response, it went to voice mail. She left a message: "*Sue, this is Joan. Call me when you get this.*"

"Ok. When you talk to her tell her that Ron is driving down to see her tonight." He turned and walked to the door. "It's time they got this mess worked out."

"Yes, that would be good," Joan agreed.

CHAPTER 69

S ue Conner walked down to meet Greg Sommers at the entrance to her dorm. He was waiting for her. She was wearing a knee length red dress with a matching blouse and red mid heel shoes. She carried a white sweater in case it got cold. Greg was wearing a three-piece gray suit with a solid blue tie. They both looked appropriate for the concert crowd.

"Wow, you are really beautiful," he said.

"You are early," Sue said as she greeted Greg.

"Yeah, it is a long drive, I want to get there early," he replied. They walked out to his car.

"Wow," she said when she saw his car. "You have a Cadillac Escalade?"

"Yeah, I like the larger SUV size," he explained. He opened the door for her. Then he started the car and they drove north on the city street.

"I thought we were headed south?" Sue asked as she recognized that the direction was toward Cleveland, not Cincinnati.

"I am taking a short cut to the interstate," he explained.

Sue was confused but shrugged it off. She took this opportunity to check the text message she had received. (*'Sue: I didn't send the message to you about breaking up. I think we have been hacked. I am driving down to see you tonight. I love you, Ron.'*). She was speechless. She turned to Greg. "Greg, please turn around. I need to return to the dorm."

"What about the concert?" he asked.

"I really need to get back right away, I'm sorry." Sue pleaded.

"It's too late now," he said loudly. Suddenly a hand from someone who had been hiding in the back seat reached forward with a taser instrument and shocked Sue on the neck. She immediately went stiff and lost all control of her body. She did not understand what had happened. She was still conscious but could not talk or move. Greg pulled off the road with his four-way flashers on. Sue saw a hand from behind her give Greg a syringe. He raised her skirt a couple of inches and inserted the syringe and injected her in the thigh. She felt a warmth travel from her leg to her head. Her vision went blurry and she felt dizzy. Then everything went black. Greg turned back onto the road and continued to drive north.

CHAPTER 70

JUNE

It was about 9:30 when Ron drove onto the campus. He pulled into the parking lot at Sue's dormitory and parked his jeep. He had traveled over the speed limit all of the way but had been lucky in not getting a ticket. He got out and ran to the door, then ran upstairs. The hall monitor told him that the curfew time was almost up and that he would have to leave. He ignored her and ran to Sue and Joan's door. He knocked hard on the door. Joan answered the door. The hall monitor was calling the police. She thought it could be the killer attacking someone in the dorm.

"Ron!" Joan exclaimed as she opened the door.

"Where is Sue?" he shouted as he rushed by her. He scanned the room but Sue was not here.

"She left on a date with Greg. They are going to a concert. She should be back soon." Joan was glad to see Ron. She never really believed that he could be so mean as his fake text messages made him out to be.

"Can you call her?" he asked.

"I already did but it went to voice messaging."

"I sent her a text but I think she must have ignored it since it was from me," Ron groaned.

Just then policeman Andy Hall came through the door with his gun drawn. He lowered it when he saw it was Ron.

"What's going on?" Andy asked.

"I needed to talk to Sue, sorry that I was so late." Ron looked at Andy.

"I thought you guys split?"

"Yeah that is what we thought… but apparently our phones were hacked somehow," Ron explained.

"Yeah, I wondered about that. You two were tight." Andy turned to see the hall monitor at the door. "It's Ok. He is a policeman." Andy referred to Ron's status as an auxiliary policeman. The hall monitor turned and walked away. "So where is Sue?" he asked.

"She left to go to a concert. She should be coming back soon. The doors lock at midnight." Joan answered.

"Do you mind if I wait?" Ron asked.

"No. you can stay." Joan replied. "I don't think I can sleep now anyway."

"Well, I am out of here." Andy turned to go.

"Andy…Really nice to see you again. It's been a while." Ron shook his hand.

"When you coming back to help us catch the strangler?" Andy asked as he walked to the door.

"I will come when I can," Ron answered. He turned to Joan, "Got anything to eat? I skipped supper to drive down here."

"We got some chips, some yogurt in the fridge and a can of peaches," Joan offered what she had.

"Thanks, I will pass on the yogurt but the peaches sound good." They both sat down to wait for Sue to come home.

CHAPTER 71

When Sue woke up she could not see, she was obviously blindfolded. She was in a cramped area, as her knees were bent. She did not know where she was but there was a lot of rough side to side movement. Her neck hurt and felt like bad bee sting. She could hear a loud motor and splashing. It was not a car motor, she thought. Her hands were taped together in front of her. Her legs were taped together at her ankles. The smell of this place was disgusting, it smelled like dead fish. Her stomach was in turmoil. She had a gag over her mouth but wanted to throw up. She knew if she did she would choke so she struggled not to. Her whole body hurt. Her hands were numb but she managed to reach up to her mouth and pull the tape off. She rolled on her side and threw up. Now it really did smell bad. She felt waves of nausea come over her. Then she drifted off back into unconsciousness.

CHAPTER 72

It was morning. Sunlight coming through the dorm window woke Ron up. He was at first confused, where was he? Then it all came rushing back to him. He was in Sue's dorm room. He looked around. Sue was nowhere to be seen. Joan had fallen asleep in her chair. He got up and nudged Joan.

"Where is Sue?" Ron asked.

"Whaa.." Joan opened her eyes groggily. "Didn't she come home last night?"

"Apparently not."

"Wow, she should have been home no later than midnight." Joan had a concerned look on her face. "I will call her again." She dialed Sue's number. It came up 'OUT OF SERVICE'. "Her phone must be off or damaged," Joan said.

"Well, I am going over to the police department to get an alert out." He walked to the door. "Call me if she does show up."

Ron walked over to the police department. He needed to walk so he could think. Sue is now missing. She may have been taken by the campus strangler, which means that Sue was probably dead by now. He refused to acknowledge that yet. Until she was found, there was a chance that she was alive. He wondered about this guy Greg Sommers. He had briefly met him once. He seemed to be pretty harmless. Ron walked into the police station. George was in his office.

"Hi George." Ron walked into the office.

"Hello Ron. Did you get to talk to Sue?" George looked up from his paperwork.

"No. She went out last night and never came home."

"Oh no…" George groaned. "Not Sue."

"She went to a concert with a guy named Greg Sommers. She didn't come back." "Is he a student?"

"I believe so. He is in two of Sue and Joan's classes." Ron looked at George with an angry look.

"Maybe She went home with him?" George postulated.

"I suppose it's possible, but I doubt it."

"Let me look him up." George stated using his computer. He had access to the campus housing directory. "Here he is." He pointed to an address in one of the dormitories. "Let's go over there and check it out. It's the Sanford dormitory." They walked out to the patrol car. George drove through the campus to the Sanford Dormitory. They parked the car and entered the building. George lead Ron up the stairs to the third floor. As they approached room 315, George unholstered his weapon and knocked on the door. "Campus Police, open up," he shouted. There was no answer. He tried the door but it was locked.

"I guess I can get a key from the manager" George said.

"No…I want to open it now." Ron said as he kicked the door in.

"OK." George entered the room and looked around, his pistol still out. Ron entered and started looking around also.

"Well, they are not here," Ron stated the obvious.

"It is possible that they may have both been kidnapped," George wondered. He started to search the room. He looked in the closet. "Oh no," he exclaimed.

"What is it?" Ron asked. He looked where George was pointing. There, on the floor were three women's purses and several rolls of gray tape.

George picked up one of the purses. It was Barbara Perry's. He picked up another one. It belonged to Cindy Carson. Both were victims of the campus strangler. Just to make sure he picked up the third purse.

It belonged to Patty Sinclair, the third victim. "Oh my god." George looked at Ron.

"We now know who the campus strangler is."

"Yeah…and he is with Sue right now." Ron's voice trembled. He stumbled over to the bed and sat down.

George got on the phone. He called the city detectives to get their forensic team over to Sanford Hall. Then he called Andy Hall and told his team to check what kind of car was registered to Greg Sommers and then put an all-points bulletin out on his car. He also called the FBI and told them that a Susan Conner had been kidnapped by the campus strangler. He looked at Ron who was in shock.

"Come on Ron, we have work to do."

"She is dead, isn't she. That is his MO, he grabs the girls, rapes them and then kills them." Ron had tears running down his face.

"We don't know that," George said. "We might catch him before…" He did not complete the statement.

"Yeah. I got to go and tell Joan." Ron walked out of the room.

"Are you staying for the weekend?" George asked.

"I'm not going back to Cleveland." Ron answered as he walked down the hall. When he left the dorm and started to walk to Joan's dorm, he got out his cell phone and called Jeff Tyler at Newmatics.

"Hello Jeff," he started.

"Ron. How are you doing? I hear the test was a great success. I was hoping to see you in the office this morning."

"Ah…Jeff?" Ron asked.

"Yes, what is it?"

"I need some time off. I know I don't have any accumulated vacation time but this is an emergency," Ron replied in a low voice.

"What has happened?"

"My girlfriend at the college has been abducted and I need to work with the police here," Ron explained.

"Oh boy…I am sorry to hear that. Sure, take as much time as you need," Jeff replied.

"Thanks. I will work twice as hard when I get back, honest."

"Don't worry about it, Ron.. You are our star engineer. Just make sure you come back."

"Thanks." Ron hung up. He wondered just how long they would let him be absent. Ron kept walking until he got to Joan's dormitory. As he approached, he saw Joan walk out of the door. She saw Ron approaching.

"Hi Ron, is there any news?" Joan asked. "I am going to the Student Union to get breakfast."

"Joan, can you sit down with me for a minute?" he motioned to a nearby bench.

"What is it?" She was getting concerned.

"We found out who the campus strangler is," he started.

"Oh good. Maybe we can get back to normal now." She brightened a bit.

"Joan...It is Greg Sommers."

"What!" she exclaimed. "It can't be...We have been with him in several classes this semester, he has been really nice..." Then she realized that Sue was with Greg last night. "No..." she began to cry. "Not Sue. Not our Sue."

"I am afraid it is true." He started to cry also. They hugged each other.

They stayed together like that for a while and then walked together to the Student Union where Ron bought them both breakfast. As they sat and ate in silence, Joan finally started talking.

"You know, Sue dated Greg a couple of times in high school but then she terminated the relationship. She never told me why, but I got the impression that he was overly aggressive toward her."

"It is possible that he became obsessed with her," Ron postulated.

"Then why kill all of the other girls?"

"I don't know. I just don't know," Ron replied.

Jerry, Joan's boyfriend walked into the Student Union and saw Ron and Joan sitting together. He walked over to their table and joined them.

"Hi Ron. Long time no see," he studied their sad faces. "What's wrong?"

"Susan has been abducted by the campus strangler," Joan said in a flood of tears.

"Oh my God…No…No, that can't be true," Jerry said.

"I'm afraid It's true," Ron replied. He wiped a tear away. "I have to go to the police station."

Jerry came around and hugged Joan as she continued to weep for her best friend. Ron left them and walked over to the police station.

CHAPTER 73

JUNE

S ue woke up again. Her mouth wasn't covered. But she still had the
blindfold on. She managed to remove the blindfold with her taped
together hands. It was dark but she could tell that she was in a small the
hold of what was probably a boat. It was probably the box fishermen
threw their fish into after being caught. It had stopped moving which
is what probably made her wake up. She started to work at the tape
around her hands with her teeth. Suddenly the hatch above her opened.

"So, the bitch is awake," a female voice sounded. The influx of
light after being in the dark blinded Sue. She thought the voice was
familiar somehow. As her eyes adjusted, she recognized the woman as
the one that was naked topless in the break-up text from Ron.

"It's you," Sue stated.

"Ewwe... You puked in there." Penny held her nose. "You will have
to clean that up."

"Why are you doing this to me?" Sue asked.

"For some reason Greg needs you. By the way... your boyfriend is
really sexy but I couldn't get him interested in me. He is the first man I
ever couldn't seduce. He must really love you a lot. So, since I couldn't
seduce him I had to trick him."

"How...?" Sue asked.

"Oh that. Your boyfriend is a brilliant, fantastic engineer but he has a tendency to leave his phone unattended when he is out of his office. That part was easy," Penny explained.

"So, you sent the message."

"Yes and I had your number replaced with one of my own and then blocked your original number," Penny bragged. "It was so easy to turn him against you."

"Can you please cut this tape off?" Sue held up her hands.

"Yeah, maybe later." Penny took the taser and stuck it against Sue's thigh and zapped her. Sue was instantly immobilized. She then got another syringe stuck in her leg. Everything started to turn dark. Sue passed out again.

CHAPTER 74

George Coleman was in his office in the campus police department. Ron was sitting across from him. George had just answered the phone and was writing down some information. He looked intently at Ron.

"What is it? Ron asked.

"That was the city forensic office. The DNA found in Greg Sommers apartment is an exact match to that of the DNA found on all three victims. Greg Sommers is our murderer."

"I was afraid of that. Greg knew Sue from high school." Ron looked down. "I suppose we should be looking for her body now." Ron was starting to cry.

"We have everyone looking in the wooded areas around campus. If he keeps his MO we should find her soon," George stated, depressed. "At least now we know who he is and we will find him, I promise you that."

"I want to help you do just that," Ron said with anger in his voice.

George knew that Ron was too close to this investigation due to his relationship with Sue, but he could not deny his best friend a chance for revenge. Ron was still an auxiliary member of the campus police force and should be included in the investigation. They would track down this murdering monster. George had already contacted the Bureau of Motor Vehicles to trace what type of car Greg drove and its license number. It was a Cadillac Escalade. He had put out an all- points bulletin in Ohio and adjacent states to find the car (and hopefully Greg Sommers). So far there were no sightings of his vehicle. They had put a watch on his dorm room just in case Greg returned to it.

The FBI were getting involved since this was obviously another kidnapping. They had started to transmit data on Greg Sommers to George and the city police.

"Did you know that Greg is a Canadian citizen?" George was reading some of the data he received.

"Really? I didn't know that, but I didn't really get to know him much from the one time I met him. He seemed to be alright to me but apparently he is a psychopath," Ron replied. He remembered meeting Greg in the Student Union when he stopped to see Sue after class. Sue introduced Greg as a student from her high school graduating class.

"Yes, I agree. He immigrated to the USA when his parents moved here from Montreal. His father made a lot of money as a plastic surgeon then moved his family to the Cleveland area." George read further. "His father had a business partner, Jaques Fortrain, who also moved to the Cleveland area. They made a lot of money and then quit their practice in Canada to move to the states."

"Maybe we can contact his parents to find out where he might be hiding," Ron suggested.

"That's a good idea. I will get right on it," George agreed.

So far the police had not found Sue's body. They had searched all of the wooded areas around the college campus and even looked in the city park but found nothing. Ron decided to go over to Sue's dormitory and talk to Joan. He said goodbye to George and walked to the dorm. It was a warm sunny day for the beginning of June. Today was the last day of spring semester and a lot of students were packing up and preparing to go home for the summer. Ron remembered that it was the start of the summer semester in June last year that he had first met Sue Conner. He was taking a couple of summer courses so he could graduate at the end of the fall semester. He had initially seen her in the Student Union and thought she was the most beautiful girl he had ever seen. Although too shy to approach her directly, it turned out that they were both taking freshman Psychology. She was taking it since she was a freshman. Ron was taking it to complete a required number of elective courses. He ended up sitting next to Sue in the class and they began a friendly conversation that eventually led them to start dating. Later he had asked her to marry him and she had accepted. That was all in the past now. He figured she was dead but somehow he could not accept it yet. Some instinct told him that she was still alive somewhere. Ron walked up to the dorm and started up the stairs. He knocked on Joan's door and she opened it. Jerry, her boyfriend from a local fraternity was there also. He had been dating Joan off and on for several months and it appeared that their relationship was progressing.

"Hi Jerry," Ron greeted him.

"Have you heard anything yet?" Joan asked Ron. She was extremely saddened by her best friend being the fourth victim of the campus strangler.

"Nothing yet." Ron sat down in the chair by her desk. He was obviously depressed.

"Maybe she's still alive!" Jerry interjected. "Didn't you tell me that they dated in high school?" Jerry asked Joan. "Could it be that he is secretly in love with her."

"We can hope that, but why did he kill three other women? His DNA was a match to what was found on the other three victims." Ron replied.

"Oh…I didn't know that." Jerry looked at the floor.

"Just keep it to yourself for now. That fact was not released yet," Ron warned.

"But it is still possible that she is alive?" Joan pleaded.

"I can only pray that she is," Ron said depressed, "Can you remember anything else from the other night about Sue's date?" he asked Joan.

"No, all she said was that they were going to go to a concert and she was happy to be going out again. She had been terribly depressed the last few weeks due to the break-up. I think it will probably affect her grades this semester since she hardly studied at all," Joan replied.

"I don't think we will worry about her grades at this point," Ron said. We are going to report her as being kidnapped to the FBI, that may help us find her if…she is still alive". Tears ran down his face. "I have been such an idiot. I should have known that she wouldn't split up with me. I thought that it was her option to quit the relationship and I respected her wishes."

"When she tried to call you, she found that her number was blocked," Joan explained. And when she called your office, the secretary said that you were out of town and were planning on marrying someone else."

"The secretary said that?" Ron was shocked. His mind raced. Could it be Penny?

CHAPTER 75

Sue woke up slowly. She was dizzy. She was spread eagled on her back on what felt to be a bed. Her head hurt. She felt nauseous but had nothing left to throw up in her stomach. She had a blindfold on so she couldn't see. She tried to move her arms but they were both secured to the bed posts, and her feet were also secured the same way. So, she basically couldn't move. Then she had a horrifying discovery. She was totally naked, but covered with a lightweight blanket. She struggled to move but couldn't. It was quiet but there was a low rumble sound in the background that could be a generator. What the hell had happened to her? She remembered being shocked, and being in something that could have been a boat. Yes, there was a woman that shocked her. She began to remember that the woman had explained to her how she had engineered the break up with Ron. But why was this happening to her? She thought that they were going to a concert and then everything turned into a nightmare. Maybe this was all a bad dream? But it felt real. She had no idea what time or day it was but she was really thirsty. The nausea covered up the hunger she probably should be feeling. Suddenly she heard footsteps approaching.

"Hello?" she asked.

"Well…Sleeping Beauty awakes." It was a female voice, the same one as before.

"Can you help me? I need to go to the bathroom," Sue asked.

"Great." The reply was in a disgusted voice. "I am not going to do all this scut work for him. He will have to do some of this himself." She walked away.

"Please wait…Please?" Sue pleaded.

"Ok, let's do this," the female voice stated as she walked back to Sue. The blanket was removed. "Ok. Lift your butt." She placed the bedpan under Sue's abdomen. "At least you didn't puke again," the female voice said.

"Thanks. Can you remove the blindfold?" Sue asked.

"I guess it wouldn't hurt." She removed the blindfold.

"Thanks," she looked at her tormenter. It was the same beautiful girl she had seen on the boat, the same one who had been semi-naked in the text that Ron sent. Only now she knew that Ron had not sent it. "Why are you doing this to me?" Sue asked.

"Hey, it's nothing personal. I am helping my brother to achieve his big obsession."

"Greg? Greg is your brother?"

"Yeah, he is my younger brother. We are a team and have been working together for years," the woman replied. She removed the bed pan and made a face, obviously disgusted with the contents. She set it on the floor.

"What obsession?"

"He was smitten with you in high school, wants to own and possess you. Forever."

"Oh my god." Sue was shocked.

"Yeah, I guess he tried a few others but they were not pleasing him so he killed them."

"He's the strangler!" Sue exclaimed.

"I suppose you could call him that. If you are smart and want to stay alive you better do what he wants. We've gone to a lot of trouble to get you here."

"Where are we?" Sue asked.

"Someplace where no one will ever look for you."

"What is your name?"

"You can call me Penny," the woman replied. "I am only here to help out for a while, then I am going to fly to the Bahamas for a well-deserved vacation." She used some toilet paper to clean Sue's butt, then re-covered Sue with the blanket.

"Where is Greg?" Sue asked, looking around. The room appeared to be a large sized bedroom with windows letting light in from behind her.

"Oh, he went to the mainland to get supplies," Penny answered.

"The mainland?"

"Oh, I probably shouldn't have said that... but it probably won't matter. We are on an island. There is no escape. The water moves past the island really fast. If you were to jump in the water it would sweep you away rapidly and smash you upon the rocks downstream."

"We were on a boat?" Sue remembered the movement she experienced in the dark hold.

"Yep. But don't worry, I will be using it to leave after Greg gets established here."

"I guess I still don't understand."

"You will be spending the rest of your life here, one way or another. All of the police back in Ohio will figure that your body is so well hidden that they will eventually give you up for dead. That is why he killed all of those other girls and hid them in the woods."

"Ron won't give up on me," Sue said defiantly.

"Oh, he is in California running some tests. He will soon forget all about you," Penny lied.

"How do you know?"

"I was the executive secretary that arranged his flights and hotel. I was working at Newmatics with your boyfriend but I don't have to go back there now," Penny answered. "I was supposed to seduce your fiancé but he has a strange loyalty to you. So, I had to trick you two into splitting up so Greg could eventually try to date you.

"You tried to seduce Ron?" Sue was interested.

"Yeah...but he would have nothing to do with me. I never have any problem with seducing men. With him it was very strange. I really couldn't get him interested. But now I am free and don't have to go back to that job."

"You are giving up a good job?" Sue asked.

"Ha ha…Greg and I are independently wealthy; we don't need any jobs. Greg arranged all that and I helped him," Penny laughed. "We inherited millions when our parents were killed."

"Sue was confused. Please, may I have drink of water?"

"Sure." Penny got a water bottle with a straw and let Sue sip some of it.

"Not too much," Penny took the bottle away. "We don't want to have to use the bedpan again until it is washed out."

"Thanks. How about something to eat? I am really hungry," Sue asked.

"No. That is part of the plan. If you aren't nice to Greg he doesn't feed you."

"Please, just a snack?" Sue pleaded.

"Sorry. I have to take care of this." Penny picked up the bedpan and walked into what appeared to be a bathroom connected to the bedroom. She heard water running, a toilet flush. Then Penny walked out of the bathroom. She walked over to Sue.

"Well, good luck to you. I hope you start liking my brother. Otherwise, he may kill you too." She walked to the door and closed it behind her.

CHAPTER 76

Ron was with George in the campus police station. Sue's body still had not yet been found. The police were still looking at all of the possible places around the campus. Ron and George were looking at a campus map with areas that were already searched highlighted and marked off.

"Do you think he has changed his pattern?" George asked Ron.

"I don't know, but possibly he hasn't killed her yet. At least I hope not." Ron hoped.

"I was looking into Greg Sommer's parents. Apparently they died in a house fire four years ago," George informed Ron. So, the only family Greg has in Ohio is an older sister. I tried to contact her but she doesn't go by the name of Sommers anymore. She apparently got married and now her last name is Webber."

"Wait a minute…What is her first name?" Ron asked.

"Penelope, Penelope Webber." George replied.

"Son of a gun! The secretary where I work is named Penny Webber," Ron exclaimed. "She must have been the one that hacked into my phone. Joan said that when Sue tried to contact me at work the secretary said I was getting ready to marry someone else."

"That is interesting. That seems more than a coincidence."

"Yeah. I guess she started there just before I did." Ron remembered the conversations with his instrument guy, Gary.

"Well, another strange thing is that her husband died in an apartment fire about two years after they got married. She got a large insurance policy payoff," George said. And that was about the time that her parents also died in a fire."

"Well, that was convenient for her. I think she tried to seduce me a couple of times but I couldn't take the bait because of my commitment to Sue."

"I looked into what classes Greg was taking this last semester. It turns out that although he registered for the Fall Semester, he did not register for the Spring Semester." George looked at Ron. "I thought Joan said that he was in her and Sue's Math and Accounting class?"

"So... he was just going to class to be near Sue?" Ron asked.

"That must be it. Why else would he attend two classes that he wasn't registered for?"

"This is starting to look like a big conspiracy just to get to Sue," Ron said, exasperated.

"I agree. The fact that your phone was hacked and you were removed from the situation allowed Greg Sommers to get close to Sue and be in position to date her. But he didn't want to date her, he wanted to abduct her. But why did he kill the other three women?" George asked.

"Either he is a complex maniac or a psychopath." Ron stated.

CHAPTER 77

S ue was still laying on the bed. It was getting dark outside. She had not seen either Penny or Greg for the last four hours. She was really getting hungry now. Her stomach hurt badly. She began to think that they had abandoned her. She was still covered by the blanket. With nothing else to do she had worked on trying to get her arms and legs free. She had managed to loosen the rope on her right foot slightly so she started to concentrate on it. It was loosening but she still could not get it free. She heard footsteps approaching so she stopped pulling on the rope.

"Well, what prize do we have here?" It was Greg Sommers.

"Greg? Why are you doing this?" Sue asked looking at him.

"Well, you rejected me in high school. You were the most beautiful girl in the senior class and you rejected my advances to you. But I was fascinated by you. You were the nicest, most perfect female I had ever met. So, I decided to get you and possess you," he explained.

"I thought we were friends. You didn't have to do this," Sue pleaded.

"You rejected me!" he shouted and pulled the blanket off her, exposing her nakedness.

"Please don't," she pleaded.

"I could take you right now and there isn't anything you could do about it. But I'm not going to do that. You will have to beg me to make love to you." He grinned.

"That's not going to happen," she replied.

"Yes you will. Otherwise, you will starve to death. Every time we make love you will gain a little bit more freedom." He came over and fondled her breasts. "You want me yet?"

"NEVER!" she shouted, turning her head away from him.

"OK. We will see. I can wait." He threw the blanket at her and walked out.

Sue started to cry. Why was he so cruel? Why had he abducted her? She had dated him a couple times in high school but she wouldn't let him take advantage of her. When he called for another date she said she was busy. She tried to avoid him at school and she thought he sort of got the message. Then in college she thought he had matured since he acted friendly and did not pressure her for a date. She thought hard about what Penny had told her about causing the breakup with Ron. Was this all a complex plan to get to her? She could not imagine why they would go to so much trouble to get to her. She missed Ron. She hoped that Ron would come and find her and free her from this maniac. She still loved him and hoped he still loved her. She kept working at the binding on her right foot. Sometime during the night, she managed to free her right leg. The rope had cut into her ankle and it was badly cut and was sore. But it was free finally. She fell into a troubled sleep. She was very hungry but still fell asleep.

CHAPTER 78

Ron woke up from a troubled sleep in his campus apartment. He showered and dressed and decided to go for breakfast. He walked down the street to the nearby diner and had a ham and egg omelet with a large glass of orange juice. He wondered where Sue was and hoped she was ok. He paid and left for the police department. George was already in the office. He had called the Cleveland Police to ask about the fire that killed Greg Sommer's parents. The detective he talked to transferred him to the officer who investigated the deaths.

"Hello?" Sargent Frayer answered.

"Hello. I am Police Chief Coleman and I was hoping to talk to you about some deaths that occurred about three years ago. Do you remember the fire at the Phillippe Sommer's house?"

"Ahh...Yes that was a strange case."

"Why do you say that?" George was curious.

"Well, the couple were in bed and even though the smoke alarm sounded they did not get up. It was a loud one and the neighbor who was sleeping with her window open distinctly heard it. After the upstairs fire was put out by the fire department, we examined the bodies and they both had fractured skulls. There was a golf club on the floor, although the rest of the golf equipment was in a downstairs closet. The fire was basically confined to the upstairs."

"That must have made you wonder if it was a murder," George replied.

"Yeah but the doors were locked from the inside, the firemen had to break it down to gain entry. The fire marshal found evidence that they were smoking in bed so claimed it was an accident."

"Where were their children?" George asked.

"The married daughter was at her apartment with her husband and the son was visiting her that night. So, they had alibis," the Sargent replied.

"Still, that sounds suspicious."

"That's not half of it. The next night a similar fire occurred on the other side of town. A Canadian doctor and his wife died in almost a similar manner. Again, a golf club was found on the floor of their bedroom. They did not have any children."

"What was the name of the doctor?" George inquired.

"Ahh…wait a minute, I have to look it up. Ok, here it is…Mr. and Mrs. Jaques Fortrain."

"Really? That was the partner of Phillippe Sommers when they had a practice in Montreal."

"Wow…that is a coincidence. I didn't know they were connected," Sargent Frayer noted.

"Yeah, and now it turns out that the Sommer's son Greg is a mass murderer. He killed three women on our college campus," George replied.

"Hey, I heard about that. With their parents dead the two Sommers kids inherited about five million dollars. You think maybe the kid did in his own parents?"

"I think that is a definite possibility. He appears to be a psychopath. Can you look up something else for me?" George asked.

"I suppose so. What is it?"

"There was an apartment fire that the Sommer's daughter lost her husband in. Name was Webber," George explained.

"I don't have any information on that…let me look it up." The Sargent turned to his computer. In a couple of minutes, he came back on the line. "Ok, I found it. The husband was at home watching a football game when he somehow lost consciousness. Then he died when a grease fire in the kitchen burned the apartment. The fire marshal concluded that he was overcome by the fumes. A neighbor thought she saw a young man leave the apartment about 15 minutes before the fire was reported, but she couldn't provide any details. The man's wife was out of town, vacationing in the Bahamas with her girlfriend. As I understand it she had a quarter million dollar life insurance policy on her hubby. The neighbor said that they argued a lot."

"Wow," George sighed. "What if the brother-in-law came over to watch football, knocked out Webber and then set a pan of grease on the stove on high before he left?"

"Jesus. The kid would have to be a ruthless psychopath to do that."

"Yeah," George agreed. He thanked the Sargent and hung up.

Ron had entered the office and heard most of the conversation on George's speaker phone.

"George, this kid sounds like our killer, striking again to make his sister rich," Ron speculated.

"But they already had five million from the death of their parents, why not just get a divorce?" George questioned.

"Getting a payoff from the insurance was probably easier than a divorce. Besides, they had already killed twice. What's one more?" Ron explained. "Also, using a fire to cover your tracks works pretty well."

"What bothers me is why did they have to kill his dad's business partner? There has to be a reason to do that." George was puzzled.

"There must have been a good reason. They apparently killed for money until Greg started to do it here for sport." Ron reasoned. "Maybe some holdings they shared in Canada?" Ron continued to speculate.

"Let me contact someone I know in Canada to see what type of business they had. I thought they were plastic surgeons. Do plastic surgeons make a lot of money?" George wondered out loud.

Ron was thinking to himself. This guy is a real monster. I doubt if Sue can protect herself against someone so evil. He began to think that maybe she was already dead.

CHAPTER 79

Sun came shining in the window. It was early morning when Sue woke up. She did not know where she was or how she got there. She did know that she was very hungry and thirsty. She was still tied to the bed. Her foot was sore but at least she could move her leg. She waited patiently for someone to come. Maybe that was part of the plan, to immobilize her so she couldn't do anything except think. She remembered something from the psychology class she had taken last summer. Something called the Stockholm Syndrome, where the captive begins to see the point or agree with their captor after a period of time. She was determined not to let that happen to her. She would hate Greg for separating her from Ron, no matter what. She wondered if she could keep it that way after a few months. If he did not feed her at all, she might starve to death. Maybe that would be better than submitting to him. She figured that he would lose his patience and rape her anyway. There was nothing she could do about that in her present circumstance. She heard footsteps approaching. It was Greg and he was carrying a tray table and a plate of hot food. It smelled delicious. He pulled up a chair and sat down facing her. Maybe he had changed his mind about feeding her, she thought. He sat down and began to eat in front of her. It was scrambled eggs, bacon and toast.

"Hello, Beautiful," he said between mouthfuls.

"Are you serious about starving me?" she asked.

"All you have to do is be nice to me and let me make love to you and I will whip up another batch," he replied.

"Go to hell," she said turning her head away so she didn't have to watch him.

"Ok, but this is really good."

Sue began to think that maybe she could trick him. It was worth a try. "Ok," she said, "but I want to eat first."

"No…You don't want to make love on a full stomach." He put the food down and got up and started to lower his pants. Then he started to crawl onto the end of the bed with his privates exposed. She took her free foot and kicked him as hard as she could in the groin.

"GAAA…" Greg screamed as he rolled onto the floor in a fetal position.

"How's that," she screamed at him. "You feel better now?"

"You rotten bitch," he groaned, still rolling on the floor. "God… that hurts." He limped out of the room slowly mumbling "You rotten bitch" over and over. She figured he was down for a while. The plate of food was still near her bed. Maybe she could get free and get something to eat. She desperately tried to get free. Now that her right leg was free, she could roll to her left. It was a strain on her right arm but she could just reach the bonds holding her left arm with her teeth. She chewed at the rope. It was hurting her mouth but she kept at it until finally she got it loose.

Now she had one hand and one arm. Her hand was numb since the blood supply was cut off by the rope. She shook it, trying to get blood back into it. Then she tried to turn as far as possible to her right. Her left hand just barely reached the bonds on her right hand. She pulled and tugged at the knot, finally after about 15 minutes she got it loosened. Now she had two hands and a foot. She gradually bent over and worked on the binding on her left leg. These were easier than the ones on her hands and she freed her foot. She now could get off the bed. She was a little dizzy from all the exertion and not eating for two days but she went and sat in the chair and devoured the now cool meal. It tasted delicious, even cold. She consumed every scrap of food, but was thirsty. She went into the bathroom. Her cup with the straw was there on a sink that had a faucet. She turned it slowly to fill the water glass, then drank down the contents. It tasted a little rusty but she did not care. She realized she was still naked so she looked around for some clothes. There was a closet in the bedroom and she found her clothes hanging on a hanger. She quickly dressed but there were no shoes. Where were her shoes? Oh well, it didn't matter. She had to get outside to freedom and raise the alarm. She looked around for a weapon in case Greg returned but could see nothing that would work. In her karate training she had been taught to improvise but she needed something more than a plastic cup or a wire clothes hanger. She did not know how much time had passed since she had kicked Greg. It seemed a long time ago. She just had to get out of this house. She tip-toed out of the doorway and along a corridor. A couple of other doors connected to the corridor but they were closed. She did not want to open them in case Greg was in one of the rooms. There was a large curving stairway that led to the first floor. She started down the stairway, trying not to make any noise. The house was an old style Victorian, probably built in the early 1900s, she thought. She reached the bottom and looked around.

CHAPTER 80

Ron was in the police station, sharing some donuts with patrolman Andy Hall.

"We searched all over campus but could not find any trace of Sue," Andy explained. "That Greg guy never returned to his dorm room. He must be staying somewhere off campus."

"I am thinking that he is on the run and probably holding Sue as a hostage." Ron took another bite of a donut.

"I hope he comes back; I would like to beat on him with this," he held up his police baton.

"Not if I get my hands on him first," Ron growled.

"Ron! Come here." George motioned to him to enter the office.

Ron entered and sat down. "What is it?"

"I just had a call from the FBI. They located Greg Sommer's Cadillac Escalade."

"Where was it?" Ron was getting excited.

"They located it in a parking lot at Hopkins Airport in Cleveland." George replied. "Do you think he flew somewhere?"

"If he did there will be a record of where he flew to. We need to contact airport security." Ron replied.

"But if he did, where is Sue? Do you think she went with him?"

"I doubt that she would agree to do that," Ron answered. Can you look up his sister Penny's BMV records to see what kind of car she drives?"

"I can do that." George started to type on his computer keyboard. "Here it is. She has a new BMW and an older mini-van."

"Put an APB on the van if you can. They could use that type of vehicle to transfer a hostage,"

"Is that what you think?" George asked.

It's a guess, but I don't think they are flying anywhere."

"Ok. I will put out an alert," George agreed.

The phone rang. It was George's friend Jim Dubois, who was in the Canadian Mounted Police. He and George had met at a police conference a few years ago. They had shared some stories and become fast friends. Jim had made some official inquiries into the history of the Sommers family with his Mountie friends in Montreal. Geoge put it on speaker.

"It turns out that Dr. Sommers had inherited a large tract of land near Montreal. He had a very successful practice and made a lot of money doing plastic surgery but wanted to retire early and move to the States. He decided to sell the land. His partner wanted to move to the States also but didn't have the funds. It turns out that Dr. Sommers partner had inherited an island in the St. Lawrence Seaway. So, he sold half of his island to Dr. Sommers. I understand that the Sommers family spent a couple of summers on the island. Then later they all moved to the USA," Jim related.

"Thanks a lot Jim." We really appreciate it. "By the way, where is this Island?"

"Oh…It is in the St. Lawrence Seaway north of Montreal. It is called the Island of Despair."

"Why do they call it that?" George asked.

"Well, according to an old Indian legend curse, everyone who tries to live there dies violently."

"Wow. Well Jim, thanks anyway."

"Ok. You owe me one." He hung up.

"They own an island?" Ron was amazed.

"Dr. Sommers and his wife apparently died violently, so maybe there is something to the curse?" George laughed.

"If both doctors owned half of the island and one of them died, the other could take the whole island over by simply paying the taxes for the entire island," Ron speculated. "So, Greg probably now owns an island."

"How does that help us?" George asked.

"Where would be the perfect hiding place for him?"

"An island in a foreign country?" George smiled.

"Yes." Ron brightened up, "Maybe he took Sue there."

"Why would he do that? He killed the other three girls."

"Yeah but we have not found her body. Maybe she is still alive," Ron was hoping out loud.

"You really think she is on a Canadian island? Are you nuts?"

"Can you think of any other reason that Greg would kill his father's partner?" Ron asked.

"We don't have any evidence that he did," George replied.

"Stop thinking like a cop. It all fits together, don't you see?" Ron pleaded.

CHAPTER 81

S ue looked around. The stairway was near a door to the outside.
She wanted to explore the house but was afraid she would run into
Greg and he probably had a taser. She didn't want to be shocked again.
She carefully went to the door and opened it slowly. There was a set of
steps that ended at a gravel path. She carefully closed the door behind
her and walked onto the gravel.

"Ouch." Her feet hurt from the gravel. She needed shoes. She
stepped off the gravel and walked in the grass next to the gravel path.
She looked back at the house. It was an old mansion type building.
She wondered if she should follow the path. There were not many
options, she thought, so she followed the path. There were large trees
everywhere, broken up by a few large boulders. She hurried down the
path, afraid that Greg would come after her. She had to find someone
and get help. It was a warm sunny late June day, probably in the 70's
she thought. She followed the path as it slanted downward. She could
hear rushing water ahead. She turned a corner and saw that there was
water rushing by. She neared the edge of a cliff. The gravel path ended
at a wooden dock. Steps went down to a platform. This would be where
a boat would dock but it wasn't here. Maybe that meant that Penny was
gone. If she was on an island like Penny said, it was in a wide river. She
could see large transport boats moving past near the other shore. She
wondered if she could swim to the other shore. The water rushing past

was awful fast. She doubted that she could fight against the current. Maybe the other side would be easier. She turned around and followed the path back toward the old house. She did not know that she had tripped a motion detector. Greg had spent a small fortune in setting up a series of security cameras and motion detectors on the island. As she neared the house, she got away from the path and started to go around the house. Her feet hurt more as she tried to cut through the undergrowth. She sort of hopped from place to place as her feet got pierced by the coating of pine needles and sharp weeds and pine cones and plant growth that was away from the path. She sat down under a tree. Her feet hurt and were bloody. She heard something behind her but before she could turn around she felt the familiar taser shock. She went stiff and her teeth bit her tongue. Instead of a momentary shock, this time it continued for a longer time. She shook with the shock. Her mouth started to foam. Then everything went black.

CHAPTER 82

Ron and George were in a meeting with FBI Special Agent Chuck Farmer in George's office. It had been two weeks since Sue had been abducted. The FBI were of the opinion that Greg Sommers had most probably buried Sue Conner somewhere and then left the country. The fact that his expensive Cadillac Escalade was left at the airport tended to support the FBI theory. However, no airport records or ticket sales showed that he had bought a ticket and flown away. No airport video records showed him on the concourse to the flight gates. The FBI figured he had probably used a false passport and a disguise to board a flight and leave the state. He certainly had sufficient funds to pull that off. Ron still refused to believe that Sue had been killed.

A check of Penelope Webber's employment at the Newmatic company showed that she had not shown up for work since Sue had been abducted. The campus police were convinced now that she was an accomplice to her brother Greg. The further investigation into the fire deaths of their parents now looked like homicides. The FBI had used drones to search all sections of the campus but not found any body or evidence of a possible burial. So, they believed that Greg had disposed of the body outside of the campus, although they did agree there was a small possibility that she was alive and being held captive. What surprised them in this kidnapping was that there was no message asking for a ransom. They did not know the actual reason that Sue was abducted.

"So, we are basically at a dead end," Chuck Farmer stated. "The city police were looking for possible burial sites in the city but it is a big city.

"I believe that Sue is still alive," Ron replied.

"What do you base that on?" Farmer asked.

"I just can't feel that she is gone," Ron looked him in the eye.

"Well, that certainly is a scientific evaluation," Farmer commented.

"I would like to assume that she is alive until we know otherwise," George interjected. Just then the phone on George's desk rang. He picked it up and said hello. "It's for you." He handed the receiver to Farmer.

"Yeah…" He said into the receiver. He listened for a minute. "Ok… Thanks. He hung up. Farmer turned to George. "You asked us to find a mini-van belonging to a Penelope Webber. It's been found. It was found in Plattsburg, New York. Actually, the local police found it since it was parked at a marina and apparently abandoned.

"Is that off of Lake Ontario?" George asked.

"No, it is near Lake Champlain.

"This Greg guy is a Canadian citizen, right?" Farmer asked. "Could be he stole a boat and went to Canada."

"Or had a boat already there waiting for him," Ron added.

"Sounds like we need to make a trip to New York." George looked at Ron.

"We really don't have any positive evidence that his sister Penelope helped him. She could just be trying to decoy us away from her brother," Farmer hypothesized.

"Well, we have no leads here so…" George smiled.

"Ok, but keep me informed of what you are doing. We don't want any international incidents." Farmer walked out of the office.

"Ron, I want you to pack a bag and bring your pistol."

"We are going armed into New York?" Ron looked at George.

"Hey we are police officers doing an investigation. You still have your badge, right?"

"Yes," Ron smiled. "How about we go in my Jeep Wrangler so we don't have any static from the campus for using one of the college patrol cars?"

"Sounds good," George replied. "Let's meet here tomorrow morning at 7 am. I will put Andy Hall in charge of the police force here."

CHAPTER 83

JUNE

Sue woke up on the bed. She was face down with her head turned away from the door. She was immediately aware of pain. Her back felt as if it was on fire. Her mouth was sore. Her feet were sore. She was amazed to see that she still had her clothes on. Her hands were not bound. She tried to turn on her side. Her feet felt to be restrained but she could move them. She turned and sat up. Her sore feet were bandaged but there was a thick steel ankle bracelet on each leg with a short chain connecting them. A third chain was attached to the center of the chain between her legs by a padlock. She followed where this chain went and saw that it was connected to a large metal panel on the wall by a heavy bracket. So, she could get up and walk around but only as far as the chain would let her. Her feet were tender from all of the cuts from going without shoes but she could walk slowly with some pain. The shackles limited her step size. The chain was long enough to enable her to hobble to the bathroom. She used this opportunity to use the toilet. There was a mirror over the sink. She got up and raised her dress up so she could see her back. She could see two distinct burn marks on her back where the taser electrodes had struck her. She also noticed there was a leather collar around her neck with a steel ring attached, probably for a chain attachment. She was being chained like a dog. The very thought of it was repellant. She did not deserve to be treated this way. It was dehumanizing. She hobbled back over to the bed and sat down. She noticed a red light on a sensor above the door that flashed red when she moved. It was a motion detector. She had not noticed it before.

"Hello." Greg limped through the door holding a cane. He had the taser in his other hand. "Sorry about the shackles but I don't think I can take another kick in the nuts," he smiled.

"Why are you doing this to me? Please let me go," Sue pleaded.

"Can't do that. Not after all the trouble it took to get you," Greg grinned.

"Why…why is it so important to ruin my life?"

"Not ruining it…just changing it so that you can be with me and not that Ron fellow."

"I love Ron, not you. You are a terrible person. Did you really kill those girls?"

"Watch what you say. Yes, I killed them since they weren't you," Greg frowned. "I want to show you something. Hold still." He attached a leash to her collar but was holding the taser in his hand. "Please don't make me use this." He handed her a key and told her to unlock the padlock on her shackles. Sue thought about karate chopping him but with the taser so close she decided not to. She unlocked the padlock and gave him back the key. He backed away as if he knew he was too close, holding the taser pointed at her. He pulled on her leash and they walked down the hall to the room at the end of the hall. He opened the door and led her inside. She was amazed. There were dozens of TV monitors and a bank of motion detection lights with a placement sign under each giving a location. "You can see that there is no place you can go on this island without me knowing it."

"So… you saw me escape," she noted.

"Yes, but you slowed me down a lot when you assaulted me. I waited for you to get close to where I was hiding. I am sorry if I had the voltage set too long but I had to make sure you were immobilized. I really do not want to hurt you but you made me do it."

"Why is it so important that you hold me as a prisoner?" she asked.

"It won't always be that way. Once you accept the inevitable we can have a happy life together." He smiled at her.

"I can never be happy with you."

"We will see. The first year will be hard but you will come around." He smiled again.

"Where is your sister? Is she going to help you brainwash me?"

"Probably on her way to the Bahamas by now," he stated. "You must be hungry; we should go down to the kitchen and I will get you something to eat."

"I thought you were going to starve me into submission?" Sue asked.

"Penny warned me that it would not work. We will live simply until you come around. Besides, you've made it difficult for me to make love for a while."

"I am sure that Ron will come to rescue me," Sue said defiantly.

"You better hope not, since then I will be forced to kill him. Besides, he will never know where to look. This place is a perfect hiding place," Greg bragged. "This is an island that no one knows about back in Ohio."

"Where are we?" she asked. She realized it was an island but where?

"We are no longer in the United States. Since all of the other girls were killed and hidden in the woods, the police will assume the same has happened to you. They will search for your body for quite a while as the trail here gets colder by the day."

"You really think I will start to like you?" she asked.

"Oh, it may take a few months or even a year but eventually you will accept your fate here," he smiled. "I can be a charming host if I want to be. We can share good times or you can suffer, it is up to you."

"Good times? Isolated from the world here?" she asked incredulously.

"Yes. Remember that as you become friendlier, your freedom will be gradually restored."

"I wanted a career…teaching children, not suffering with some maniac on an island."

"Be careful of what you say," he pointed the taser at her. "You will still be able to teach children…our children." She was shocked by this revelation. Was she supposed to bear children for this monster? He was sicker than she thought.

CHAPTER 84

Ron and Geroge were leaning over his desk looking at a map of Canada. Based upon the latitude and longitude coordinates provided by George's Canadian Mountie friend, they found the island in the Saint Lawrence Seaway just north east of Montreal. On the map it was just a small speck, hardly worth any notice.

"You really think that is where he is hiding?" Ron asked.

"Well, it looks like a perfect hiding place. If it wasn't for my friend we would never have thought of looking there." George put his finger on the map.

"How do we get there?" Ron asked.

"Probably by boat," George suggested.

"Look… there are three locks between Lake Ontario and Montreal." Ron pointed at the map. "At each stage you would be inspected and even though you are a police chief, the Canadian border guards won't let you in with a weapon."

"We have to use the same route that he used to avoid detection. Remember that the sister's car was found near Lake Champlain. We need to start there."

"That's got to be an eight hour drive at least," Ron figured.

"We need to get started soon then. Did you pack a bag?"

"Yes, I also have both of my pistols, The browning nine millimeter and the small .380."

"You still have that old antique and that little pop gun?" George held up his 17-round Glock, a policeman's weapon. "Come on, we need to get going."

They took turns driving while listening to the greatest hits of the Eagles DVD. After a while it got to be too much and George turned it off.

"Is that the only disk you brought?" George asked.

"Well, it is my favorite," Ron admitted.

"Most of those songs are 40 years old. How about something newer?" George asked.

"If we stop at a rest stop you can buy a Taylor Swift DVD, OK?

"Ha, Ha, Ha," George laughed.

CHAPTER 85

S ue sat at the table looking at the grilled cheese sandwich Greg gave
her. It was burned on one side. He obviously was not a good cook.
She thought about her situation. She might as well make the best of
it until the cavalry arrived. She had no doubt that Ron would keep
looking for her. But she was tired of getting tasered every day. She
would pretend to be nice to Greg, maybe he would eventually give her
an opening that she could take advantage of and put him down. She was
a trained 3rd degree karate blackbelt and knew several ways to disable
another person. All she needed was a chance. Unfortunately, Greg
knew how captives thought. He had studied all about the Stockholm
Syndrome and knew that she would start being friendly until she had a
chance to ambush him. So, he acted accordingly. After lunch, he took
her back up to her bedroom and chained her to the wall.

"Take a look in the closet," her told her.

She went to the closet and opened it. There was a bunch of dresses,
skirts and other clothes hanging in there. She noticed a lot of items
were her size.

"How did you know what to buy?" she asked.

"Penny picked out all that stuff. She seemed to know what size you
were."

"Well, that's nice, but how do I change clothes with this chain on?"
she said, pointing to her feet.

"We will work that out later. Right now, I have to go downstairs. Try to entertain yourself." He pointed to a bookshelf with some books on it.

"Gee, thanks," she said, glad that he was leaving. After he left she looked around the room for something she could use as a weapon. The room was incredibly bare. She looked at the window. It appeared to be sealed shut. The view was fabulous though. The house was high on a hill so that she could look over the trees and see blue water. Off to the side she saw a cargo ship traveling past the island although it was about 200 yards away toward the other side of the river. The day was clear and the sun was shining. It was getting warm outside and there did not appear to be any air conditioning in the house. She tried to pull the chain off the wall socket but it was very strong and she couldn't budge it. She walked to the door and tried to open it but it was locked. Living here was going to be boring she figured. She needed to escape.

CHAPTER 86

Ron and George drove Interstate Route 90 to New York and then cut north on Interstate 87, arriving at Plattsburgh Boat Basin mid-morning after driving all day and night. They had stopped for gas and meals. They did stop at a truck stop for a short 3-hour nap in the car. George had a AAA map of the area so they navigated their way to the Plattsburgh Boat Basin. It was a large marina on Lake Champlain. They got out and walked around. The Marina office was apparently in the Ships Store. They entered the store and walked up to the counter.

"Hi guys, you checking out a boat?" a tall guy wearing a T-shirt, jeans and a baseball hat asked them. He had a clipboard in his hand.

"Hello." George showed the man his badge. "Can I ask you a few questions?"

"Ah…OK." He put the clipboard down and looked at George. "That doesn't look like a local police badge. Where you fellas from?"

"My name is George Coleman and this is my deputy, Ron Pritchard. We are from Ohio. We would appreciate your helping us track a killer."

"My name is Chad. I'm the manager here. What can I do for you?"

"Can you see if you had a boat stored here for a Greg Sommers or a Penny Webber?"

"Let me check…" He walked over to a desk with a list of boat slips. He scanned the list. "Yes, there was a cabin cruiser stored here by a Greg Sommers. I remember him, he paid a year in advance to tie up to one of our slips. He also paid for the boat to be stored in the marina during the winter. We cover them with plastic and store them on shore in one of the boat houses."

"Is the boat still here?" Ron asked.

"Well, that's the strange part. We typically don't have people check out boats at night. But they came in after midnight and took their boat out on the lake. Not a safe thing to do at night," Chad responded. "I told them it was against the rules but he gave me a hundred dollar bill and said that rules don't apply to him."

"When was that?" Ron asked.

"Geeze...that must have been almost two weeks ago. And what is even weirder, they did not come back," Chad explained. "And their boat was painted black. Most of the boats are white so people can see them in the dark or fog. Very unusual."

"I have to ask... is Lake Champlain connected somehow to the St. Lawrence Seaway?" Ron asked.

"Well, not really. But...if you go to the north end of the lake there is a small canal that is used for transportation to the Seaway, but it is monitored closely by the border patrol," Chad remembered.

"Could a cabin cruiser, painted black, sneak through there during the dark?" George asked.

"I suppose it is possible. If they motored up there from here at top speed they would get to the canal around 4 AM. The guards would not be on alert at that time in the morning, I suppose."

"Thanks," George replied.

"Anything else I can do for you?" Chad asked.

"No, not really. Is there a sporting goods store in the area?" George asked.

"Sure, there are couple on Bridge Street, about two blocks from here."

"We appreciate your help. Thanks." George turned to leave.

When they got back outside, Ron turned to George. "What do we do now?" Ron asked.

"First thing, let's get a good lunch and find a hotel for the night." He turned and looked at the adjacent restaurant, 'The Naked Turtle'. "Let's try this place." They went in and had a couple of burgers and beers. While they ate George explained his plan. They would buy a small kayak and sneak through the canal at night and then paddle to the island. Ron was skeptical of this plan but he didn't have any better ideas.

"Look, if we get there and the place is deserted, we can check in with the Canadian Mounties to see if they have any ideas." George explained. "At least we know he was here. If they came at night they could have snuck Sue on board without anyone seeing them."

"Yeah, we came this far at least we can try this." Ron agreed. He looked up and saw Chad had entered and sat at the bar. He looked over and saw Ron and George. He walked over to their table.

"One other thing," Chad said as they looked at him. "This Greg guy had this really hot chick with him and they carried an awful lot of stuff on to their boat. One thing even looked like a rolled-up mattress."

"Are you sure it was a mattress?" Ron asked.

"I don't know. The broad was talking to me while he was loading the boat. She was a real looker," Chad explained.

"That was probably Penny." Ron said.

"Well, hope you guys find him." Chad turned and walked back to his seat.

"This is starting to make sense," George said as they ate their meal.

"The mattress could have been a body, maybe Sue," Ron said excitedly.

"Either that or a dead body that would be easier to dispose of on the lake," George said grimly. That got him a sharp look from Ron, but they had to consider all possibilities.

Afterward they drove over to the sporting goods store. George seemed to know what he wanted so Ron just followed. The store had a few fiberglass kayaks and some inflatables. George was talking to a store salesman and told him what he wanted.

"We don't have any of those on display but I have one in the back storeroom that might be close." The salesman lead him to the back of the store. They went through a door and there were several boxes piled up and they walked through a maze of boxes until they were next to the back door. A large 3-person kayak was on a rack. It was a plastic covered inflatable built on a fiberglass frame. It had three seats in series and came with three double-ended paddles. It was white with blue accents. A name on the side said Kodiak. It was 13 feet long.

"We don't get much call for these; they are basically out of style. This is the last one I have left," the sales person noted.

"Can a small motor be attached to it?" George asked.

"Well, we don't have those, but I know a guy that can mount one of those electric motors on it." He wrote down a phone number and gave it to George. "The kayak is $800."

"We will take it." George agreed. "Ron, give him your credit card."

"Wha…" Ron protested for a second then shrugged and pulled out his wallet. They pulled Ron's Jeep around to the back door and mounted the kayak on his roof with some bungee cords. George called the phone number and a guy named Taylor said he could provide what George was asking, for a price. They drove over to his house and he had a shop in the back yard. After some negotiation, he showed them a 3-HP electric motor that could be mounted to the kayak with a bracket. It would cost them about a thousand dollars and they would have to leave it with him overnight. George agreed. He gave Taylor two hundred dollars in cash for a down payment and they left to find a hotel for the night. Since George had given most of his cash to Taylor, they had to stop at a bank so Ron could withdraw some cash using his debit card. They found a Comfort Inn and got two rooms. Ron was tired from all of the driving and a long hot shower really felt good. He took a small nap and then met with George and they drove to a Texas Roadhouse they had seen while driving to the hotel. They had a good steak meal and headed back to the hotel.

'You think we have to paddle all of the way up to the St. Lawrence River from here?" Ron asked George as they drove to the hotel.

"No, I looked at the map before we left to go eat. We get back on route 87 and drive to Rouse Point, just below the border. We find a secluded place to put into the Richelieu River and head north. We do it at night and pull off the river during the day, hide in the woods. I figure we can get to the Seaway in about three days, only paddling at night. I don't want to get caught by the border patrol."

"Ok. Sounds like a plan. We will need to buy supplies and stuff."

"Yeah. I am glad you have your credit card," George smiled.

CHAPTER 87

S ue had been trying to be a good girl so Greg wouldn't get angry at
her. She only spoke when he spoke to her and then in only a low
subdued voice. Greg knew that she was being submissive so that he
would get careless around her. So, he played along, trying to be nice to
her but not letting his guard down. He had fixed chicken noodle soup
by heating up a couple of cans. Sue thought to herself, If I am forced
to live here, he better start letting me cook the food. She told him that
she needed a bath and asked politely to have the ankle shackles off.
She was amazed that he said Ok. They went up to her room and he
gave her the key, always holding the taser in a threatening way. Then
he left the room and locked the door. She celebrated her freedom by
practicing several karate kicks. Then she took a nice hot bath, washing
up for the first time in a week. Afterward she noticed it was getting
dark outside. There was no clock in the room so she didn't know what
time it was or even what day it was. When she was drugged, she had no
concept of how much time it took to get here or where here even was.
She remembered being on a boat, but was that on the Great Lakes? He
said they were no longer in the United States so most probably that
meant Canada. If she was in Canada, what river was in Canada? She
was not familiar with what was north of Minnesota. If they had gone
east, how did they get around Niagara Falls? When she was a child she
remembered crossing the Peace Bridge to visit Niagara Falls with her

family. She knew that there were locks at Windsor to get around the falls. She doubted that a boat would go that way without an inspection by the border police. If they inspected the boat she would have been found. It was possible she supposed that since he was rich (according to what Penny told her) maybe he paid off the inspectors. That thought depressed her. She would have hoped that men responsible for stopping smuggling would not be easy to bribe. It was getting darker. There was a light on the ceiling but there was no switch by the door to turn it on. As it got darker she crawled into bed and went into a troubled sleep. It was so nice not to have the shackles on. She dreamed of Ron coming to rescue her but when he was gunned down by Greg, she woke with a start. Now it was really dark. She could see nothing so she turned on her side and went back to sleep.

CHAPTER 88

Ron and George checked out of the hotel. It was nice to get a full night's sleep. They made several stops. They bought camp food supplies and stopped at the sporting goods store and bought wetsuits, black of course. They stopped at a hardware store and bought flat black spray paint.

"What are we going to use that for? Ron asked.

"You will see," George said.

They drove over to Taylor's place and knocked on the door to the workshop. Taylor opened up the door and greeted them. "I just finished charging the batteries for you." He showed them the bracket he had put on the back of the kayak. The engine just fit into the back storage compartment. "You will have to have the batteries near your feet, so don't let the boat turn over. Do you know how to right a kayak if it turns over?" he asked.

"I was a boy scout," George related. "We had several lessons before we were allowed to kayak on the Ohio River."

"Ok then. This boat is somewhat more stable than a single kayak." Taylor showed George how to mount the motor and connect the battery. "It should last at least five hours at the full speed setting. You will need to use your paddle as a rudder though."

"Sounds good. How much do we owe you?" George asked. After they paid him and mounted the kayak on the Jeep, Ron turned to George. "You know that was about the last of the money in my checking account."

"Will it be worth it to you if we find Sue?" George asked.

"Ok. I will shut up," Ron admitted. They got in the Jeep and drove north to Rouse Point, near the border. George was driving and he pulled off at a rest stop. Ron looked and they didn't need gas.

"Why are we stopping?"

"You will see." George got out of the jeep and retrieved the black paint cans. He turned to the kayak and began spraying with the black paint. Ron got the idea and sprayed the other side of the kayak. Now it was totally flat black and none of the external original color showed.

They then covered the kayak with a tarp so no one would notice an all-black kayak. They got back in the Jeep and drove to Rouse Point. They got there in time for lunch so they stopped at a small pizza joint to get something to eat.

George explained the plan to Ron. They would wait for darkness and find someplace to put the kayak in the water. Then they would sneak under the bridge to enter the Richelieu River. The bridge was technically the border between Canada and the USA. There would be a patrol boat but they would hug the shore and quietly paddle downstream. With any luck they would get by.

"If we get caught?" Ron asked.

"We got lost and turned the wrong way in the dark. We show them our badges and tell them we are on the trail of a killer. With some luck they might let us get back to the USA."

"Or they lock us up and alert the American authorities that they caught some armed Americans trying to illegally enter Canada," Ron answered.

"Hey, it's worth a try," George replied.

"Ok. You are right," Ron agreed.

They drove into town and checked out a place called Barcomb's Marina. They saw a border police car parked in the lot so they just drove by. They drove around the town. George saw a dog park that was close to the shore near the bridge. He realized that no one would be there around 2AM walking their dog. The parking lot was close to the river. It was about perfect except there was a 10-foot fence at the rear of the park. They would deal with that later. They drove around until they found a small park. They got out and walked around discussing their strategy. They had to wait a few hours until it got dark. They returned to the Jeep and decided to take a nap in the truck. George opted for the back seat. Ron stayed in the driver's seat but put the seat all the way back.

They woke up around supper time and decided to walk to a local restaurant. They found a place called Best Friends Restaurant and had a meal. They both used the restroom since they did not know how long they would be on the river. As they left, it was starting to get dark. "Just a few more hours," George said as they walked back to the Jeep. When the got there, they saw the kayak was gone. What the hell? They looked all around the area but didn't see anything.

They got in the Jeep and started to drive around. Ron was beginning to get upset. All their plans were no good now. They turned down the next street and there it was. Two teenagers were trying to carry it down the sidewalk, but were tired and had stopped to catch their breath. Ron crept up on them and parked the Jeep. George got out of the car and approached them. They saw him approach and started to run but ran right into Ron. He grabbed them and dragged them over to George. They were very young only about 12 or 13 years old. George pulled out his badge and showed them.

"You know you could go to prison for grand larceny?" he asked.

"We are sorry, honest...we don't want to go to prison," they answered. But then one of them kicked Ron in the shin and he released them in a howl of pain. When they took the opportunity to run down the street George laughed.

"Let them go. We got our boat back." They lifted the wrapped kayak and tied it back on the roof of the Jeep. Just then a police car came down the street and stopped by their Jeep.

"Having a problem?" the policeman asked as he rolled down his window.

"No, Officer, just adjusting the load." Ron answered.

"Just what do you have there?" the officer asked.

"It's just a canoe. We were planning to head upstream tomorrow toward Plattsburgh, maybe do some fishing."

"You have Ohio plates. Are you visiting someone in the area?" the policeman asked.

"We are police officers just taking a vacation in your wonderful state." George took out his badge and showed him.

"This says you are a police chief," the officer stated as he handed it back.

"Hey, everyone needs a vacation," George replied.

"Ok. Just checking. Have a wonderful trip." The police car drove off.

"You think we fooled him?" Ron asked.

"Well right now he is checking us on his police band computer to see if we are legit," George assured Ron. They drove back to the main highway and parked behind the pizza place they had lunch at.

"Might as well have another nap." George set his smart watch alarm for 1 AM.

CHAPTER 89

S ue was slowly getting used to the monotony of her existence here with Greg. They did the same thing every day. He would unlock the door and make sure she was dressed. Then have her lock her shackles on and follow him downstairs for a breakfast, usually cereal or pancakes with sausages. Then he would lead her back upstairs and lock her in her room until noon for lunch.

This process was repeated at dinner time but sometimes he would let her into the front room to watch a movie on a TV that had a DVD player. Typically, they were old movies that she had already seen but any change in the day to day tedium was appreciated. He would always sit behind her with the taser ready. Then afterward he would ask her how she liked the movie and try to discuss it with her. She would answer in monosyllables. She had no desire to discuss anything with him. She hoped he would get tired of her and maybe decide to let her go. He understood what she was doing, she was entering phase two of the Stockholm Syndrome. He smiled and led her back upstairs. Soon she would start to come around and start to want to be near him. The solitary confinement between meals would eventually make her desire human contact and if he was all that was available, she would start to like him. Once she started to like him they would move on to closer intimacy and then sexual satisfaction. He just had to be patient. He was almost totally recovered from her kick now so he wanted to hurry the process but knew she had to take her time.

Sue was trying to survive. She had no idea when Greg would stop acting nice and simply attack her. She tried to be alert and look for an opening to use her karate. Unfortunately, her feet were shackled with the chain and about 80 percent of karate involves kicking. She had not been able to find a useable weapon anywhere Greg let her go. She knew they had been at the island for almost two weeks. What if Ron never came to rescue her? She was horrified that she may be stuck here for quite some time. Penny had told her that she was unable to seduce Ron so she used his phone to send erroneous messages to split them up. What if Ron still believed that Sue did not want him anymore? He was up in Cleveland. He might not even know she was missing. She was sure that George would tell Ron. Or at least she hoped so.

CHAPTER 90

Ron and George were at the dog park. It was deserted and the whole town was apparently asleep. It was warm but cloudy but the moon was hidden by clouds so it was very dark. They had changed into the black wetsuits. They carried the kayak to the back fence. George walked along the fence and found a spot where it could be lifted enough to slide the kayak under. They made several trips back to the Jeep and stored their supplies in the middle seat of the 3-person boat. Then they snuck under the fence and pushed the kayak toward the river. No one was around and no one saw them. They slid the kayak into the river and paddled under the bridge and into the Richelieu River. They stayed near the shore and tried to be quiet.

They did see a patrol boat but it was docked at the other side of the river. They proceeded down the river in the dark. The clouds separated a bit and there was enough light for them to see the shore and try to stay in the middle of the river. They paddled all night and when it started to get light they searched for a good spot to pull over and get out of the kayak. There were a lot of forest areas to choose from but they wanted a relatively deserted area without any houses around. They finally found a suitable spot and pulled over. George checked his GPS meter and they had made good progress. They had passed Saint-Paul-de-I'lle-aux-Noix and had found a small camping area. They brought the kayak ashore and secured it to a tree. They set up a small tent at the bottom of a hill and had a snack of beef jerky and peanut butter on crackers. They had brought enough water to last them about a week. It was nap time so they entered the tent and went to sleep. Ron set his phone alarm to wake them up in five hours. He was a little sore from paddling the kayak. But he was tired and had no trouble falling asleep.

Five hours later they woke up and had a noon meal and watched the river. George walked up the hill to scout the area. It was a camping area and he didn't want to run into any other campers. They were lucky, there were no people camping in the immediate area although he did see some tents about a hundred yards away. George and Ron's camp was out of sight but you never knew if someone wanted to go down to the river. He considered leaving the area during the daylight but decided it would be better if no one saw them, just in case their visit to the island turned out bad. They stayed where they were and waited for darkness. When it got dark they shared some more snacks and loaded up the kayak and pushed the boat into the water. They were still wearing their black wetsuits and were almost invisible in the dark. There were lights along the shore so they headed to the middle of the river where they would be less visible. There was a city ahead and they passed a marina where several boats were lit up. They could hear music playing across the water. Obviously some people were partying. They did not see any other boats in the river so they just kept on paddling. After a while the city lights were behind them. It got dark again with only the occasional light on the shore.

"How come we don't use the motor?" Ron asked. "I'm getting tired of paddling."

"Ron, this river is mostly calm and the current is going the same way we are. When we get to the Seaway, we will be going against the current and that is when we will need the motor," George answered.

"Ok. I guess that makes sense," Ron replied. Then they heard a motor boat approaching from the north. Since it was dark, the boat had a light on it. George who was sitting in the front figured the boat would try to stay in the center of the river so he started paddling quickly toward the shore. When the boat got close, he stopped paddling. And crouched down. Ron got the hint and crouched down also. The boat went by and there was no sign that the kayak had been seen.

They kept paddling until morning. This time there wasn't any forest along the shore. All they saw was a suburban area. People's houses lined the river on both sides. Some places had docks with boats tied up.

"What do we do now?" Ron asked.

"Just keep paddling until we see someplace to pull over and rest."

"Ok." Ron watched the shore intently. It was still early in the day, not too many people were out and about. No one seemed to notice them quietly paddling along. The river was getting much narrower. Finally, they saw some woods off to the west. They stopped and pulled the kayak out of the river and hid among the trees. George consulted his GPS and found that they were near the start of the narrow canal. He definitely wanted to transverse the narrow canal at dark since it was only about fifty yards wide. They set up camp and ate breakfast. George again scouted the woods but found that it was just thick forest. He was satisfied that if they moved far enough inland they would not be spotted. After a meal, they both settled down for good nap.

They woke up in the late afternoon. So far no one had seen them either on shore or on the river. They risked a small fire to cook a hot meal. According to the GPS they should get to the Seaway sometime near dawn tomorrow. If Greg Sommers came this way in his black painted power boat, he probably made the trip in one night. George had considered renting a boat and doing the same thing, but figured that he and Ron would probably be stopped by the border patrol. For all he knew, Greg Sommers might have been stopped by the patrol but he probably could bribe his way through or if he had a custom hiding place in the boat, the border patrol might not find an unconscious body. Also, since Greg and his sister were Canadian citizens, they might have gotten easier treatment to start with. George was much more sure of his stealthy approach.

It got fairly dark around 10 PM but George wanted to traverse the narrow canal around midnight so they waited. It started to rain. George was happy. The rain would further mask their travel up through the canal. They were now glad that they were wearing the wetsuits. They put the kayak in the river and started to paddle. The kayak started to fill with water but was still buoyant enough to keep them afloat. As the rain got harder it began to be difficult to see the edges of the canal but they kept going. The rain let up around 3 AM but still continued lightly. As it got lighter near dawn they saw the canal begin to get wider and then they were in the Seaway.

The current was much greater moving toward the ocean but they turned into the current and set up the electric motor. George started the motor and with the small motor and by paddling they were able to make headway against the current. The electric motor was completely silent so it did not make noise like a typical gasoline outboard engine. George knew that they did not want to be in the shipping channel so he maneuvered them toward the opposite shore. The GPS showed that they were about 35 miles from the island. They needed to keep paddling with the motor to make the best possible time. It started to get somewhat lighter but the rain still sort of hid them in the gloom. Ron was wet and miserable and was tired from all of the paddling. He was glad they had the motor, otherwise he knew they could not fight the current. After about five hours they saw a small island in the distance. After a quick check of the GPS coordinates, George knew they had found the right island. As they got closer, he could see no easy landing spots due to the cliff around the island shore. It was a small island, only about half of a mile long and 300 yards wide. It was, however, densely forested with trees and brush. Finally, they went just a little bit north of the end of the island and saw a possible landing site. They pulled in to the site and Ron jumped out and dragged the kayak on to the shore. Both Ron and George were exhausted from the ordeal. But they had made it to the island. They decided to rest up and get something to eat before heading inland to possibly find Greg Sommers. Although Ron was elated that they had finally made it, he was so tired that he fell asleep without even setting up the tent. The rain finally stopped. George did set up the tent and moved into it for a nap. He grabbed some beef jerky and ate some before he too passed out.

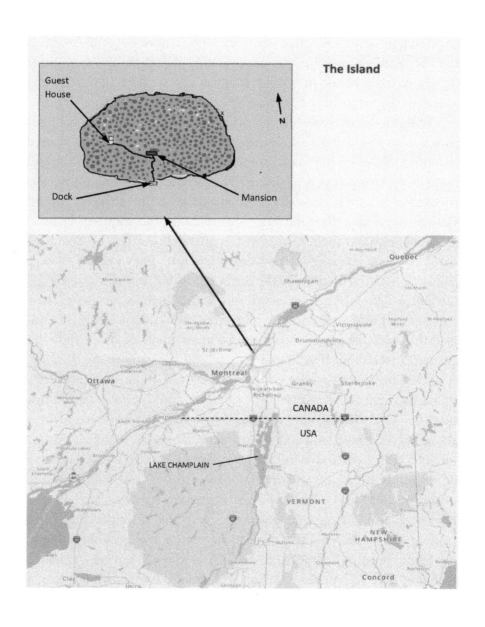

CHAPTER 91

S ue had heard the rain during the night. The lightning and thunder had awoken her and she listened to the patter of the rain on her window. Another boring day of existence. She was starting to consider suicide rather than make love to Greg, but she had nothing to use to commit suicide. There were no beams in the room to hang herself from. She had nothing sharp to cut her wrists. Her resolve was definitely weakening. She knew she would have to submit to him eventually or go mad. She really missed Ron but it looked like no one was ever going to find her. Greg was the only human she was in contact with and she needed human contact. Maybe if she was nice to him and submitted to his lust, he might give some her some freedom. She could then run down to the dock and fling herself into the river and drown. It was better than her current existence. By her reckoning she had been imprisoned for almost a month. She wondered how people in prison managed to survive. At least they were in a population. A bad population but it had to be better than solitary confinement. Her life was as good as over, she thought. As it got lighter, Greg opened the door and they went through their typical motion of unshackling her legs and she went into the bathroom to change her clothes while he watched. Then she had to re-attach the shackles on her feet and he led her downstairs for breakfast. She was chained to her chair while he cooked breakfast. Today it looked like scrambled eggs and toast. His cooking had not improved much. She offered to do the cooking but he did not trust her with kitchen utensils yet.

"How are we today?" Greg asked.

"OK."

"You ready to make love yet?"

"No." She really hated his non-romantic bluntness. He could at least try to be nicer.

"Well, you are trying my patience. But if you want to keep staying in your boring room that is your choice. You could be sharing some of the tasks I have to do to maintain this place. That is a lot better than a solitary confinement,," Greg smiled. "Eventually I will take you forcefully even if you keep denying me. I won't be very nice to you if you force me to be brutal."

CHAPTER 92

Ron awoke first. It must be close to noon he thought. He was hungry. They were on the island. Now they needed to see if Greg and Sue were here. He hoped that she was still alive. If she wasn't, he would kill Greg if he had a chance. He doubted if George would try to stop him. George woke up and looked at Ron.

"Looks like you want to get started." Greg yawned.

"Yes. Let's get this bastard."

"Ok. First we change clothes and get out of these wetsuits."

"Yeah, I really need a shower," Ron agreed.

"You can take a quick bath in the river. I'm going to. It's not that cold."

"Sounds good."

Later they dried off and dressed in police uniforms. Ron had never worn one before but did as he was told. George put on his police jacket even though it was almost 80 degrees warm. They removed their weapons from water-tight bags and made them ready. Before they started they ate some of the remaining supplies they had left and drank some bottled water.

"No good doing police work on an empty stomach," George noted.

They started working their way through the underbrush. George had seen an arial view of the island and knew the main house was at about the center of the island on the highest point. So, using his compass they headed west. Ron followed him, trying not to make too much noise.

"Oh no." George stopped. He pointed to a near tree.

"What is it?" Ron asked.

"See that trail camera over there? I think we have been spotted. If that has a live feed then we just set off an alarm."

"No need for stealth then?" Ron asked.

"No, but be prepared. We may be walking into an ambush." George drew his gun and chambered a round. Ron did the same with his Browning pistol. He had put the small .380 automatic in his back pocket as a backup. They continued forward, now at a slightly faster pace. After a few minutes they came to a clearing. They were near a path through the trees that led from a dock at the river's edge to what looked like a Victorian style mansion at the top of the hill. Everything was quiet. There were no birds singing and the wind had died down. The clouds parted and the sun was now shining.

Sue and Greg had just had their lunch. Sue was just about to agree to have sex with Greg when they heard a "Bong" that sounded through a small speaker on the ceiling.

"What was that?" Sue asked.

"Looks like we may have guests. That or a deer has swum over from the mainland. They do that occasionally. Either way, we need to get upstairs. Come on, quickly now." Sue struggled to climb the steps as fast as she could with her shackled feet. Greg was following her. She was excited, this was something different in her day to day existence. Maybe they have come to save me? Greg got to the room with all of the electronic surveillance equipment. Sue watched as he checked all of the cameras and then saw something that made her heart leap for joy. There on the camera she saw George and Ron moving through the underbrush and trees with weapons drawn. They had come to save her!

"Shit. Now I have to kill them," Greg grumbled. He pressed a button on the console. Then he opened a drawer and pulled out a nasty looking revolver and what looked like a large sharp knife. He saw that she was happy, smiling. "Don't get your hopes up. I have a secret weapon." He cocked the revolver. "This is a .44 Magnum. I can kill an elephant with this. You are going to see the damage it does to a human."

Sue was horrified. What could she do to prevent this? Her feet were still shackled. "Please let me go. I will tell them that you left for the mainland and aren't here."

"No, that won't work. We must kill them," Greg uttered. He made her hold out her hands behind her back and he taped them together.

"Please don't hurt Ron, Please, I will do whatever you want," she pleaded.

"You were about to do that anyway."

"No...I won't let you kill him." She stood in his way. At this point Greg slapped her so hard that she fell down. Her mouth was bleeding. "Get moving, Bitch." He more or less pushed her down the stairs but held on to her leash so she didn't fall all the way down. When they got to the bottom he opened the door and they watched as Ron and George walked up the path. He dragged her outside and stood behind her. She was fully dressed but did not have any shoes on. He took the knife in his left hand and put it across her bare throat and had the revolver in his right hand under her right arm. He turned her toward the approaching men.

"Stop where you are," Greg commanded as they got within about twenty feet, "or I cut her throat and you can watch her bleed to death. Drop those weapons now!"

Ron was ecstatic. His heart almost leaped out of his chest. He saw Sue finally after all these months. Her mouth was bleeding but she was still the most beautiful thing he had ever seen. He dropped his weapon as commanded. He did not want to give this maniac any reason to hurt her. George did not drop his weapon.

"If you let her go and drop your weapons I won't kill you," George said firmly.

"I will kill her and then shoot you," Greg replied. Sue wondered what Greg was stalling for. He had all of the advantage. He must be waiting for his secret weapon. Sue could not take the tension anymore. There was one thing she could do that might save Ron. She took a small step backward and quickly rammed the back of her head into Greg's face. He stumbled backward and the knife cut her throat as she dived to the side. His reaction was to pull the trigger on the 44 Magnum, but it was tangled in Sue's arm discharged harmlessly into the bushes. Greg's nose was bloody from the impact as he struggled to regain his balance.

George did not hesitate. He fired his weapon. Bang. Bang. Bang. Three bullets hit Greg in the chest and he fell backward. Ron rushed forward to Sue who was bleeding. He used his handkerchief to stem the flow of blood.

George walked over to look at Greg who had three holes in his chest and was apparently dead. Sue was smiling. "I thought you would never come. She started crying, overjoyed to see Ron. "I would never have stopped looking for you." Ron bent over her, kissing her lips.

"How sweet," a female voice replied behind him. It was Penny and she had a pump-type shotgun pointed at George. "Drop the gun." George didn't drop it but didn't point it at her either. He turned to face her.

"You killed my brother?" Penny asked.

"Yes."

"Ok." She pulled the trigger and blew George off his feet. He rolled off into the bushes. "Now I suppose I have to dispose of you two." She racked the next round into the shotgun.

"Please don't hurt us. We will let you go and won't tell the police," Ron pleaded. His hand was slowly reaching for his back pocket.

"No. I think you will. Now get out of the way so I can do her first. You know Ron, you were the only guy I ever found that I could not seduce. Is that little slut worth that much to you?'

"She is my love, my soul mate. And she is a better woman than you ever will be."

"Really? Well, she is going to be a dead soul mate. I'm going to let you watch her die before I kill you. Now move."

"No. You have to shoot me before I will let you kill her."

"Ok. Say your goodbyes." She pointed the shotgun.

"Please no...!" Sue screamed.

Just then there was another shot and Penny fell to the ground. Ron looked up. There was George standing there, holding his weapon on Penny. Penny looked up at him.

"How..." her words slurred.

"Sorry," George said as he opened his jacket and showed her his bullet proof vest. It was covered in little shotgun pellets. "You ruined my jacket."

"Bastard..." she said as she tried to raise the shotgun. George shot her again and she fell silent.

"Thanks," Ron replied as he looked at George. A couple of shotgun pellets had caught George on the face and his arm where the vest did not cover. Ron turned to Sue. The cut on her neck was not deep and was on the nape of her neck near the collar bone. It was not bleeding badly but needed bandaging.

"Let's get her unbound and go into the house." George looked at Sue. He then looked at Penny but she was dead.

"Greg has the key to these in his pocket," Sue said, pointing to the foot shackles.

"Ok." Ron went and retrieved the key and freed her. They all went in the house. After some searching they found Greg's medical cabinet and bandaged Sue's neck and George's small wounds. George was amazed at the array of electronic equipment Greg had upstairs.

"What do we do now?" Ron asked George. "Call the local Mounties?"

"I would rather not. We could get arrested for entering the country illegally and assassinating two Canadian citizens. They might not believe our story and we could be stuck for months trying to untangle this mess. Let's bury the bodies and just leave. If we are careful we can pass as Canadians until we get to a border crossing and show our badges to the US border guards. They will probably let us back into the country without too much fuss."

"Ok. All I care about is right here." He had his arms around Sue.

CHAPTER 93

Ron, Sue and George were in the house and helped themselves to food from the pantry and a hot bath. George spent some time checking out the mansion. He found a large 24 KW generator out back that provided electrical power to the house. A 1500-gallon propane tank behind the house supplied fuel for the generator. George figured it would probably last about a year before requiring a refill. How Greg had it refilled was a mystery, but Greg was a millionaire so there probably was a way. A well with an electric pump provided running water. So, the island was pretty much self sufficient except for food that had to be brought from the mainland. There was a massive pile of firewood for the three fireplaces in the house, probably to help heat the place in the winter. Ron and Sue were curious as to where Penny had come from when she was alerted of the intruders. George recalled that there was a second building in the Google maps photograph of the island he had pulled up before they had left the campus. Ron and George walked down the path to the second building while Sue searched the house for her purse and shoes. The second building was a guest house and was where Penny had been staying. It was set up pretty much the same as the mansion but on a smaller scale. The mystery of Sue's purse and shoes was solved as they were found in the guest house.

On the way back to the mansion Ron asked George, "What are we going to do with the bodies?"

"I have been thinking about that." George replied. "How about we use Greg's method of covering up his parent's murders?"

"You mean place them in the house and burn it down?"

"I checked the bodies and all of the bullets went clean through so bullets won't show up in any investigation. It will be classified as an accident," George explained.

"Also, we don't have to dig any graves," Ron agreed. "Are you sure you don't want to report all this to the authorities? It doesn't sound like something a policeman would do."

"If we weren't in a foreign country I would not do it. But we broke several laws already rescuing your girlfriend and we could be tied up in court for months."

"Look, I appreciate all of your effort and planning. It just doesn't sound like something you would do."

"I desperately wanted to get the guy that violated our peaceful campus. I would surely like to expose who and what he was, but I would rather just head home and get back to normal. I am really tired."

"What about your Mountie friend? He basically told you about this place. If it looks like something bad happened here, won't he alert the authorities?"

"Yeah, he might, but I will call him and explain what happened," George explained. They were back at the mansion. George and Ron walked down to the dock. A 24-foot cabin cruiser was tied up to the edge of the dock.

"Looks like we don't have to paddle home." George smiled.

CHAPTER 94

R on was finally alone with Sue in her prison room. She pointed out the chains she was forced to wear while a prisoner.

"Did they abuse you?" Ron asked.

"I was electro shocked and drugged most of the time until I woke up here," Sue explained. "I knew you would come and rescue me."

"We had a hard time figuring out where he would take you." Ron looked at her; she was dressed in a knee-length red dress and looked beautiful. "Everyone thought you would be dead like his other victims. But I just knew you were alive. I want you to know that I did not send the break up message."

She turned to him and smiled. "Penny told me how she hacked into your phone and sent those hurtful messages. It did not seem to be something you would do."

"I would never do that to you. I love you. If I hadn't had to go to California for a test, I would have driven down to see you right after I got the rejection message from you. Only it was Penny, not you sending it."

"She was diabolical in how she did that. She said she tried to seduce you but you rejected her." Sue looked into his eyes.

"She was beautiful, but all I could see was you and I couldn't hurt you that way," he explained. "Did Greg....?" he left the question hanging.

"Greg tried to rape me initially, but I kicked him in the groin and he stopped. After that he started to use psychology to get me to love him, but I resisted," Sue replied. "So, no, he never had sex with me." She turned to Ron and they kissed.

"Thank God," he said as they parted. "I never want to be in a situation like this again where I can't protect you." He held her in his arms.

"How did you find out about this place?" she asked.

"George was relentless in his investigation. He has a friend in the Canadian Mounted Police who provided research information on Greg's parents owning this island. It seemed logical that he would hide here," Ron explained.

"So, when do we leave to go back?" she asked.

"George and I found the boat you came here in. We probably will use that to leave but we need to clean up this place. George wants the bodies to look like they died in an accident."

"He isn't going to alert the authorities about what happened here?" She looked at Ron.

"We broke a few laws coming here. We probably should have just had the Canadian Police check this place out, but George wanted to get Greg himself. Besides, we weren't sure you would even be here."

"That doesn't sound like George. He is typically so straight about the law."

"I know, but he started to change when the girls under his protection started getting raped and killed. It became personal to him," Ron tried to explain.

"Ok. But I am so glad that you did find me," Sue smiled.

Later George filled them in on his plan. They would sleep in the mansion this night and then start out in the morning. Since the stove in the kitchen was propane fueled, he would put out the pilot light and turn on the gas. Since propane was denser than air it would accumulate on the floor. He would light a candle on the table and they would leave. When the gas level reached the candle, the house would explode and catch on fire. He would put the bodies in the bedrooms upstairs. They would leave in the cabin cruiser and tow the kayak behind the boat. Now that Sue had her purse she would be able to show her identification to re-enter the USA. When passing ships reported the house on fire, the authorities would investigate and be unable to put out the fire but would determine who the victims were. This would be on the news and George would be able to use the news report to close the case. He had it all planned out. Ron just hoped it turned out the way George said it would. Although Ron and Sue shared the same bedroom they did not consummate their reunion. Sue had not been using her birth control pills for over a month and they did not want to tempt fate.

The next day George destroyed the recorded tapes of his and Ron's entry on the island and removed the hard drives from the computers. They had recovered the kayak from the other side of the island and tied it behind the cabin cruiser. The bodies of Greg and Penny were put on the beds in the bedrooms. Susan had recovered her shoes and clothes and checked her purse. It was still intact. Even her cell phone was in it. They packed some sandwiches from the pantry and stored it in the boat. George covered the blood stains on the path with gravel. Unless you were looking for it, no one would suspect blood being there. As Ron and Sue were on the boat, Ron started the engine and checked the fuel tank. It was half full so they probably did not need to stop to purchase gasoline. While they were doing this, George setup the kitchen to explode. He came running down the path and they pulled away from the island. They traveled about a half mile downstream before George pulled the boat over into the shallows on the other side of the river from the shipping channel. He set the anchor and then they waited. After about 15 minutes they heard a loud explosion from the island and a column of smoke rising in the air. It was definitely noticeable so any passing ship should report it. At this point George had Ron puncture holes in the kayak and they watched it sink. Then they threw all of their weapons and the computer hard drives in the water. They put a Canadian flag on the stern and started their journey back the way Ron and George had come.

"Looks like the Indian legend is true." Ron told George. "Everyone who lives on that island has a violent death."

"Yeah, I suppose so." George smiled.

CHAPTER 95

They traveled back down the Richelieu River without any difficulty. As they neared the border around 5 pm, George replace the Canadian flag on the stern with an American flag. Greg had been very thorough in his outfitting the boat, George thought. As they crossed the border a patrol boat approached them and they stopped. An official boarded and did a brief search for contraband, and examined their Identification.

"What was your purpose in visiting Canada?" He asked George.

"It was just a pleasure cruise," George answered.

"Anything to declare?"

"No, we didn't do any shopping," Ron answered.

"Is this boat registered to you?" The official turned to George.

"No, it belongs to a friend, we are returning it to the Plattsburgh Marina. We know Chad there," George replied.

"Oh, Ok. I see you are in law enforcement." (George had let the official see his badge when he showed his ID.)

"Yeah, just up here on a short vacation."

"Well, you folks can go. Have a nice day." The official got back into his boat.

They returned to Rouse Point so Ron could get his Jeep. They agreed to meet at the marina in Plattsburgh. Ron was surprised to find the Jeep but there was a parking ticket on the windshield. He drove off.

George turned the boat south and headed for the marina in Plattsburgh. He and Sue reached the marina and tied up the boat. As they walked back toward the office, Chad came out and greeted them.

"You must have found your killer," Chad exclaimed. He saw that George was with a woman this time. A very pretty woman but not the one he had seen before. "Where is your friend?"

"No, we had no luck finding our suspect, but we were able to bring the boat back for the owner," George lied. "My buddy said he would meet us here." Just then Ron's Jeep pulled into the parking lot. Ron got out and walked over to them.

"Well, ok then." Chad seemed to be happy that the boat was back. "The owner paid up for the slip for the whole year."

"I am sure he will want to keep it here for now," George replied.

They all went into the Naked Turtle for dinner. Ron and Sue were happy to be together again. Ron explained how they were able to track her down. He apologized for the text messages even though he did not send them. Sue just smiled since she knew that Penny was the one that had done all that. She was happy to be with Ron again.

CHAPTER 96

AUGUST

With George and Ron switching driving on and off they drove all night and got back to the college campus around noon the next day. Ron and George had been gone almost eight days but it had been worth it, they had rescued Sue. She had slept most of the way back so she was bright and alert as they pulled into the parking lot of her college dormitory. She got out of the Jeep and ran upstairs to see Joan. She had called about an hour earlier so Joan was waiting for her. They ran to each other and hugged.

"It's so good to see you," Joan exclaimed.

"It's good to be home," Sue replied.

Ron and George stopped at the girls' room for a few minutes but the girls were occupied talking to each other, so they said their goodbyes and left for their respective residences to get some sleep. Ron called work and announced that he could return to work the next day. George stopped to visit his fiancée.

The next day George was back in the police office. A news report was received that told of an explosion on an island near Montreal. The owner of the island, a Greg Sommers, was killed in what apparently was an accident. Andy Hall already knew that Sue had been returned safely.

"I see you were busy during your vacation." Andy Hall pointed out the news article to George.

"I don't know what you mean." George replied. Then the phone rang. It was FBI Special Agent Chuck Farmer.

"I thought I told you I didn't want any international incidents," Farmer yelled.

"I guess we can close the case on the campus strangler," George replied.

"What about the last victim?" Farmer was obviously upset.

"She is back home and is ok. She wasn't kidnapped after all, but went to New York to visit some people."

"OK...I suppose everything turned out ok...but I don't condone this type of behavior from a police chief." Farmer calmed down a bit.

"It won't happen ever again," George assured him.

CHAPTER 97

George Coleman was sitting at his desk in the Campus Police Department. The phone rang. It was his friend in the Canadian Mounties.

"What the hell?" his friend Jim Dubois asked, "What did you do?"

"What do you mean?" George responded.

"I give you all that information and then the island in the St. Lawrence Seaway exploded?"

"I read that it looked like an accident." George smiled.

"Right. And you never caused it?"

"Well, look at the time it saved your police and law enforcement. You don't have to do a lot of paperwork for extradition to send him back to the States," George replied. "Besides, we confirmed the guy was our killer rapist since he left his DNA on three dead women."

"Ok. But it sure seems to be a weird coincidence."

"Did you find any evidence of our entering your country?" George asked.

"No. And I checked. But still...."

"Then it must have been an accident. I do owe you a big favor though, for the information," George tried to smooth his feathers.

"Ok. I guess I can live with that." He hung up.

George put the receiver down. He felt sort of bad about how everything turned out but he still felt justified in killing the predator on his campus. And he was happy that Susan was rescued.

EPILOGUE

L ife on the campus returned to normal. Susan was able to return to class and eventually graduated 3 years later with her Bachelor's Degree. Ron and Sue were happily married the summer after she graduated. Ron had a successful career at the Newmatic Company and eventually got a Master's Degree in Business and was promoted to be an engineering manager. They eventually moved to Strongsville, Ohio and bought a house. Sue applied for a teaching position at the local high school and taught Art. George married Jennifer and continued to be police chief on the college campus for several years. Joan and Jerry eventually graduated and also got married as Jerry became a successful salesman for a chemical company. Joan kept in contact with Sue and they often shared shopping trips together. Although the families of the three murdered coeds suffered, no one ever talked about a trip into Canada to rescue Sue.

The End

Milton Keynes UK
Ingram Content Group UK Ltd.
UKHW040654160324
439418UK00003B/35